"It was to

Caryn looked at him with something akin to shock. She shook her head slowly. "Oh, Sam, don't do that. You're too nice a man to get tangled up with me. Not to mention the fact that you really don't know me."

"You eat junk food rarely, you're a workaholic, your sense of humor needs to surface more," he said promptly. "You're beautiful, with a great figure, and your teeth are sparkling white. And basically you're a cheap date. I like that in a woman."

Caryn's eyes look incredibly sad. "If only it were that easy. I'm the first to admit I'm a complex woman, and there's no person in this world who knows me as well as they think they do. As for any kind of relationship, I just can't have one."

Sam was unperturbed. "Sure you can. You know, the more I think about it, the more I'm convinced I was sent here to loosen you up. Lady, it's a good thing I'm an expert at this."

ABOUT THE AUTHOR

Linda Randall Wisdom is a well-known name to readers of romance fiction. Long-term service in personnel, marketing and public relations gave her a wealth of experience on which to draw when creating characters. Linda knew she was destined to write romance novels when her first sale came on her wedding anniversary.

She lives in Southern California with her husband and a houseful of exotic birds.

Books by Linda Randall Wisdom

HARLEQUIN AMERICAN ROMANCE

Don't miss any of our special offers. Write to us at the following address for information on our newest releases.

Harlequin Reader Service
901 Fuhrmann Blvd., P.O. Box 1397, Buffalo, NY 14240
Canadian address: P.O. Box 603,
Fort Erie, Ont. L2A 5X3

Appearances Are Deceiving
Linda Randall Wisdom

Harlequin Books

TORONTO • NEW YORK • LONDON
AMSTERDAM • PARIS • SYDNEY • HAMBURG
STOCKHOLM • ATHENS • TOKYO • MILAN

Published May 1989

First printing March 1989

ISBN 0-373-16293-6

Chapter One

"I'm still waiting."

"I'm sorry, Mr. Russell, but as I've explained to you before, Ms. Richards is in a staff meeting, and as you have no appointment..." The receptionist shrugged, indicating her lack of power in the matter. "Ms. Richards has given orders that she isn't to be disturbed during these meetings except for an extreme emergency. Now, if you'd care to make an appointment?"

"Obviously I don't qualify as an extreme emergency." Sam exhaled as he glanced down at his watch. He had been waiting a little over an hour and a half, and by now his temper was more than a little frayed.

"Look, miss, I arrived here from Miami via what seemed to be every major city in the continental United States. I'm jet lagged, more than a little weary and in need of hot coffee, a cigarette and a hot shower, but as Mr. Gregory asked if I'd stop by here I thought I would do just that before going to my hotel. Now why don't you tell Ms. Richards I'm still here before I light up in your No Smoking lobby and spread nasty ashes all over this carpet."

"Mr. Russell, I presume?"

He turned to find a tall woman in her late twenties wearing a black leather miniskirt and black silk blouse standing in the hallway. Her artfully tousled tawny blond hair and discreet makeup finished the elegant picture. She approached him and held out her hand, speaking in a husky voice.

"I'm Caryn Richards. I apologize that you had to be kept waiting, but this has been a busy day. Would you care to come back?" She gestured down the hall.

Sam nodded but didn't return her smile. He felt much too tired to smile about anything. But he wasn't so tired he couldn't notice that she was a lovely woman. Too bad she was so tall. In her high heels she was almost eye level with him and being five foot ten himself, he wasn't fond of tall women, preferring petite ones with delicate gestures. He could see that while this woman was most definitely feminine she didn't portray the delicacy a tiny woman would.

Caryn ushered him into a large corner office that overlooked Century City and gestured to a chair on the other side of her desk.

"Would you care for some coffee or tea?"

"Coffee would be wonderful," he said quickly, salivating at the idea of the dark brew that gave him a quick start so many mornings.

Caryn placed a quick call and seated herself behind her desk. A moment later they heard a soft knock at the door and a young woman entered, carrying a tray. She set it on Caryn's desk and left.

"Cream, artificial sweetener?" Caryn asked, filling the two cups with the aromatic brew.

"No real sugar?" Sam asked with dismay.

"The staff of a health-and-fitness magazine have an image to maintain." Caryn handed him one of the cups. "I understand Mr. Gregory asked you to speak to me because of my reports."

He nodded. "I read them on the plane. You don't think it's just malicious mischief?"

She shook her head. "Maybe I'm acting paranoid, but I have a terrible feeling about this. At first I thought it was just malice on someone's part. It was nothing major, just irritating when files would suddenly disappear then reappear in the strangest places. We use a color-coding system on all our articles; red for nutrition, green for exercise and so on. We found those all mixed up one day. It took us a long time to straighten them out. So far all the incidents are minor, but I'm afraid if they go unchecked they could escalate into something harmful."

"Have you fired anyone recently? Someone who would feel the action was unjust and try to get back at you?" Sam asked, sipping the hot brew.

"No one. Our employee turnover is very low here," Caryn said, with pride tingeing her voice. "We're more than just a magazine staff, we're almost like family. It's probably because we spend so much time together."

Sam poured himself a second cup of coffee, desperately needing that rush of caffeine.

"I understand you'll be opening a West Coast office for the company's security force?" Caryn commented.

"That's right. After Mr. Gregory bought those two California-based newspapers and an Oregon-based knitting mill he decided it was time." He swallowed a yawn. "Sorry, it's been a long thirty-six hours for me. I only intended to stop by to let you know I was in town and to see if anything has happened since your last report."

"Nothing so far." Her lips twitched in a wry smile. "It makes me sound paranoid, doesn't it? We're all feeling a bit uneasy about this."

"No, you're just trying to be careful. Nothing wrong with that." Sam stood. "I'm sorry, but I'm in the need of at least twenty-four hours' sleep."

"Then I'm doubly sorry to keep you waiting. I'm afraid Lori takes her duties very seriously." Caryn also stood.

"I plan to check out my offices tomorrow. I believe they're four floors up from here. Any problem in my coming by tomorrow afternoon and speaking to members of your staff?" Sam asked, mentally comparing her chic outfit to his travel-worn jeans and charcoal wool sweater he had pulled on over his cotton shirt. He raked his fingers through sun-streaked sandy brown hair. His icy blue eyes shining out of his deeply tanned face were the only evidence of color other than his clothing. He looked her up and down, missing nothing from her black high-heeled pumps to the top of her tousled tawny blond hair. He didn't miss the amused speculation in her deep amber eyes.

"Until tomorrow, Mr. Russell." She offered her hand.

"Around two?"

"That will be fine."

Sam yawned again and chuckled. "I must be more tired than I thought. Two cups of coffee and the caffeine didn't make a dent."

Caryn's eyes danced with amusement. "Probably because the coffee was decaffeinated."

He looked dismayed. "No caffeine?"

"Not a speck."

"No smoking, no real coffee. I'm glad my office is upstairs," he muttered, walking down the hall toward the reception area. "I couldn't survive five minutes here."

"My, my, who was that?" A lovely Eurasian woman, wearing a short red dress, appeared at Caryn's side a moment later.

"Sam Russell, the head of Security for the West Coast office," Caryn replied, turning around.

"Very yummy."

Caryn laughed. "Tami, you're incorrigible. If you're not thinking about food, you're thinking about men."

"New men around here are rare. Especially one who looks as good as he does," she argued. "Although I probably should give you first dibs since you saw him first."

"You're generous to a fault." She chuckled. "Did you find that article on the new diet fads? You know the one—we were supposed to discuss it today during the meeting."

Tami grimaced, throwing her waist-length black hair over her shoulder. "Yes, this time it was my fault. I had forgotten that I had taken it home with me last night to do a final reading, and it was still in my briefcase. I should have looked there first."

"Sounds like something I've done." Caryn entered her office with Tami on her heels.

"You? Never. So, tell me more about our blue-eyed wonder." She shrugged at Caryn's questioning look. "Lori happened to mention his enthralling blue eyes. Is he going to catch our little leprechaun?"

"If he can be caught." Caryn sifted through the phone messages left on her desk by her secretary. "No one's had any luck so far."

"What are your plans for tonight?" Tami took the chair Sam recently vacated.

"Ballet class and going over everyone's weekly report, which should have been done yesterday."

"Wrong. You're going out to dinner with us," Tami informed her. She added quickly, "Come on, Caryn, you haven't gone out with us in ages. You hole up at home too much. When was the last time you went out on a date? And I mean a real date, not something that has to do with business."

Caryn sighed. "Tami, if this is going to be a lecture about my so-called lack of social activities—"

"Lack? It's called zip. If a man asks you out you firmly turn him down in such a way he wouldn't dare try again," Tami scolded. "And you rarely go out with us."

"I'm not a party animal." Her tone indicated the subject was closed.

Tami sighed. She was used to Caryn's refusals by now, but she was determined not to give up on her boss.

"All right, you're not a party animal, but it still wouldn't hurt you to go out with us tonight. We're just going to dinner."

"Tami, I have too much to do. Mr. Russell is coming back tomorrow afternoon and wants to talk to everyone about our problems, so I want my desk cleared as much as possible."

"All right, I'll give in for now." She stood up. "Well, back to the old grind."

Left alone in her office, Caryn stared down at her many messages. They would have to wait. Instead, she walked out to the lobby and made sure there was no one present when she spoke to the receptionist.

"Lori, when a man is here from the home office, you buzz me. He is definitely considered an emergency," she informed the younger woman.

Lori flushed. "I know now, Ms. Richards. Sorry."

Trying to ease the tension, Caryn said, "The only man you can buzz me for who isn't here on company business is Mel Gibson. Otherwise they have to wait."

"Sorry, if it's Mel Gibson I'll be long gone and so will he!"

"IF I HAD KNOWN I could live like this I would have taken that promotion sooner," Sam muttered, roaming through the suite at the hotel that had been reserved for him until he could find a place to live. The sitting room was furnished with ultramodern pieces as was the bedroom with its large platform bed. His first stop was the bathroom for the hot shower he had been craving while wishing there was a way to smoke at the same time without getting the cigarette wet. He called room service, requested a steak dinner and a pot of coffee, and after dining he settled in bed with his long-awaited cigarette and the reports on *Simple Fitness* magazine and its staff.

When Eliott Gregory of Wes Com bought the health magazine four years before it had been badly floundering. He made a clean sweep of the staff and brought in all new people, and when the new editor-in-chief didn't work out he promoted Caryn Richards, a features editor at that time. He told Sam he would never regret his decision, as long as Caryn did a good job and continued boosting the circulation. Now with all the problems plaguing the magazine he wondered if he hadn't made a mistake.

Sam opened another folder.

"Ah, here we are. Caryn Anne Richards, age thirty, five foot seven. Hmm, that I already figured out. Caryn, according to your performance reviews you're a regular Type A personality," he murmured, skimming the pages. "Hobbies—running, tennis, swimming. Don't you do anything sedentary?" He reached over to the night table and picked up his pack of cigarettes, pulled one out and lighted it. "You sure do a lot of investigating where physical-fitness products are concerned. No wonder the sales rose so dramatically."

He went on to the reports Caryn had filed regarding the office mischief maker. The problems hadn't begun until a little over a month ago, and since they weren't serious enough to call the police on, Caryn had merely made note of them.

The more Sam read the more impressed he grew with Caryn's sharp ability to turn a magazine around. He had guessed from the beginning that she had more going for her than her good looks. This certainly proved it. He may have been extremely tired, but he wasn't so tired he didn't miss the fact that she was a lovely woman.

"She could be a nice lady if she wasn't so tall," he muttered, just before he fell asleep as exhaustion took over.

AFTER HER BALLET CLASS Caryn headed home, wanting nothing more than a shower and change of clothing.

Wearing a rose pink sweatshirt and sweatpants over her leotard, she let herself in to her apartment and headed for her bathroom, which held a cream-colored sunken bathtub with Jacuzzi jets. After a relaxing bath, she dressed in a soft dusk-blue velour robe and went into her kitchen to make a salad.

While eating she looked through the papers she had brought home with her, but she couldn't concentrate on them because of the headache that had been plaguing her most of the day. The staff meeting hadn't gone as well as she would have liked, and Sam Russell's abrupt arrival hadn't helped any.

"Why doesn't aspirin work the way it used to?" she grumbled, trying acupressure, which also didn't seem to help the pain.

Only in the soft cocoon of her apartment did Caryn feel like her true self. At work she always wore strong colors, called "power dressing" in some circles, while her casual clothing was made up of soft pastels, as was her decor. Her cream-colored couch was piled high with pillows in ice-cream colors, the two lithographs on the walls were of hazy pastoral scenes, and a large pastel drawing of a beach scene hung over the fireplace. With classical music playing in the background, the room was a peaceful setting and altogether different than Caryn's harried working conditions in the fast-paced office with its high-tech furniture and strong color scheme. She preferred keeping her private surroundings known to few people, as if she feared they would expose her soul.

"I'VE SEEN some strange diets in my time, but this one really takes the cake," Lee told Caryn as they shared a morning cup of tea.

She smiled. "That good, huh?"

The nutrition editor wrinkled her nose in disgust. "On the first day you only eat lettuce, the second day nothing but apples, the third, any kind of melon you like and as much as you want, and the fourth anything your little heart desires, which could turn into a real pig-out considering what you can't eat the other three days. Give me a break."

Caryn chuckled. "You're right. That is definitely strange."

Lee held up a small paperback. "And this is selling like crazy because famous people swear they've lost weight on it. That's the kind of diet that will have so many harmful aftereffects."

"People will do anything to lose weight," Caryn agreed. "Are you going to discuss that one in your next column?"

"You got it. I also read about one diet—which has everything nutritional in it—that I'd like to spotlight, and the book isn't expensive, either."

Caryn nodded. "Fine." Without realizing what she was doing she rubbed her fingertips over her aching forehead.

"Headache?"

"A souvenir from yesterday's staff meeting and talking to Sam Russell."

Lee ran her fingers through her golden brown short curly hair. "It's Tami's Irish background that gives her that temper. I'm sorry, Caryn, I love her dearly, but she tends to go overboard at times. I'm just afraid she isn't going to back down this time without a fight." She showed concern for her boss. "I swear no one can throw a tantrum like her."

"Maybe so, but I'm still in charge and it's something she's going to have to remember." Caryn poured herself another cup of coffee. "I have a meeting with Mr. Russell this afternoon, so if you have thoughts on our vandal, would you please let me know before then? Although, he's going to want to talk to everyone."

Lee nodded. "I'll type up some notes for you. The sooner those Halloween tricks are stopped the happier we'll all be. Finding that goopy slime stuff in my file cabinet that morning wasn't funny to me." She glanced down at her watch. "Oops, I'm five minutes late. Our new make-over is coming in today for up-to-date photographs. She's been doing great on her diet."

"Good, I may come by to watch the shoot." Carrying her coffee cup, Caryn left the tiny kitchen two doors down from her office and walked back to her office.

"Mr. Russell called," Pat, Caryn's secretary, informed her as she walked past her desk. "He said he still planned to be here around two. I have an idea he was warning us that he doesn't work on a strict timetable. He also said he'd bring his own coffee."

Caryn smiled. "Now why doesn't that surprise me?"

Pat handed her a manila envelope. "Jay dropped off the photos he came up with for the next cover. He said his favorite is on top." She grimaced. "I confess I took a peek. Blond, long legs, high-cut bathing suit. Can't we ever use someone slightly chubby?"

"I don't think Mr. Gregory would like us to use people who aren't physically fit and healthy looking," she pointed out.

"Trust me," the secretary said dryly, "I'm sure she's had the assistance of a good plastic surgeon. If having someone suck the fat out of my thighs and taking a few tucks would leave me looking like her I'd have it done tomorrow."

Caryn opened the envelope and pulled out the eight-by-ten color glossy photographs. "Hmm, you're right," she murmured, studying the other photos. "It must have been all that milk she drank as a child. Did Jay also say why he didn't have these with him yesterday during the meeting when I wanted them? He couldn't seem to come up with an adequate excuse then."

Pat shook her head. "He said nothing except that you wanted to see the photos. But then, you know Jay. He believes the photographer is an artist and doesn't have to work on a timetable."

"No kidding." Caryn shifted her cup to her other hand. "Well, whenever Mr. Russell gets here bring him on back. I want to get this problem straightened up as soon as possible so we can stop cringing every time we walk into the office."

It didn't take Caryn long to realize that Sam's phone call was definitely a subtle warning. Although he said he'd arrive around two o'clock, it was closer to two-thirty when Pat ushered him into the office. She tightened her lips to keep back a few scratching remarks about punctuality and offered him a cool smile as he sat down in a chair holding a Styrofoam cup in one hand.

"I'm sorry you didn't like our coffee, Mr. Russell," she said politely.

He held up the cup. "The coffee was fine. It was the lack of caffeine that did me in. Coffee without caffeine is like sex without a woman."

Caryn bit down on her lower lip to keep from laughing. She might think of him as a pain in the neck, but he was turning out to be a likable pain.

"And do me a favor, call me Sam. Mr. Russell sounds so formal." He drank deeply from his cup. "I spent this morning talking to the guard downstairs discussing how security is handled after hours, and I have to tell you it's more lax than I'd like, and that will be changed immediately." His voice hardened, showing the man wasn't as easygoing as Caryn first thought.

"We have a guard in the lobby after hours and everyone is required to sign in and out," she told him. "And if he doesn't know the person, they're not allowed upstairs without proper identification or authorization."

"Wrong. That's the way it should be, but it isn't. If the night-shift guard knows you he waves you on in without having you sign the log, and one night a guy he didn't know gave him twenty bucks so he could slip upstairs and leave some roses as a surprise for his girlfriend. The man didn't come down for well over an hour."

Caryn arched an eyebrow. "Very impressive. I'm surprised he would reveal his mercenary side."

"He didn't. The stranger was one of my men I'd sent in as a test. The guard flunked and is now looking for a new job, and, without a reference, that could take some time." Sam looked at the desktop and the coffee table across the room and sighed. "I guess this is a No Smoking office like your No Smoking lobby."

"Yes, it is." There was no apology in her tone.

He leaned back in the chair looking so relaxed Caryn wouldn't have been surprised if he had fallen asleep. Dressed in neatly creased jeans and a rust wool sweater with a cream-colored shirt underneath, he looked more like a casual Yuppie instead of the head of the West Coast security office—and one of the best, according to Eliott Gregory. If he hadn't been wearing a tie, albeit a rumpled one, she would have been convinced he didn't own one.

"What exactly is your capacity here?"

"My title is editor-in-chief, but that's purely for the masthead. I do a little bit of everything. Our staff is small because we like it that way, and when things get rough everyone pitches in to get things done on time. We don't stick to our job descriptions."

He stretched out his body and crossed his legs at the ankles. "What exactly does your magazine do besides tell people to eat bean sprouts and work their fannies off so they can have perfect bodies?"

Caryn knew he was needling her, but she wasn't going to fall for his tactics. "Obviously you haven't read it. We have features on health spas all over the country, we interview fitness experts, show new exercise clothing, discuss various diets, makeup ideas. Twice a year we devote an issue to teenager fitness. We've had excellent response to those."

Sam nodded, looking sleepy-eyed. "Get them trained early, right? Good idea."

"Obviously you don't believe in taking good care of your body," Caryn said stiffly, not appreciating his brand of humor when it hit on the one thing she cared about. She considered the magazine her life, and she didn't like anyone making fun of it. As far as she was concerned it was the same as making fun of her.

He shrugged. "Caryn, I've done more traveling than an airline pilot in the past eight years. I'm usually lucky to have enough time to grab a halfway decent meal, as long as I can find a fast-food restaurant. My exercise is chasing down white-collar criminals. I might not be into Nautilus or counting calories, but I'm not a complete wreck, either. All Mr. Gregory said I had to do was figure who's causing trouble at the magazine. He didn't say anything about having to follow your fitness policies, too. He knows I'm not one to munch on carrot sticks or do one hundred sit-ups every day."

"I had an uncle who smoked four packs of cigarettes a day, drank enough Scotch to float a battleship, thought an exercise program was for wimps and believed cholesterol was merely a fancy word for all the foods he loved," she said quietly. "He died of a heart attack two years before his fortieth birthday."

Sam nodded, understanding her general concern for anyone who, in her eyes, was abusing their bodies, although he knew there were other ways to kill oneself. "My grandfather has smoked cheap cigars since he was ten, drinks moonshine, which is probably made out of rubbing alcohol, and doesn't believe his food should be cooked in anything but pure lard. He just celebrated his eighty-seventh birthday and his doctor declared him to be in perfect health, although he doesn't know how he does it. Personally I think it's because he's such an ornery old cuss."

Caryn smiled, warming her amber eyes. "It appears we're at an impasse. Shall we each declare ourselves the winner and get down to business?"

"Sounds fair to me."

She brought out a file folder. "What you've previously seen are my reports. These are notes jotted down by my people so you'll have a more personal feel for all this. Needless to say this has us all on edge. No one wants to come in to the office early, because they're not sure what they'll walk into, and no one works late without someone else staying behind. That's a rule I made after the second incident."

"Good idea." Sam nodded as he leafed through the folder. "Off the top of my head I see this as someone on a revenge kick. Anyone you've ticked off in a bad way?"

"Anyone who's written a rip-off diet book or put out faulty exercise equipment," Caryn said promptly. "And that's only the tip of the iceberg. Someone with false qualifications was running a health spa two years ago and we exposed the operation. I don't like fakes, Sam, and I'll do everything possible to make sure no one is hurt or cheated."

He ran one hand through already tousled hair as he sipped his coffee. "You're a hard lady, but obviously an honest one. No wonder your magazine does so well. Your readers know they'll get accurate information from you."

"Exactly."

Sam stood up, carrying the Styrofoam cup in one hand and the folder in the other. "Well, let's see what we can do here." He headed for the closed door.

"What exactly do you intend to do about this?" Caryn asked after him.

He turned around and flashed her a cocky grin. "Don't you fret, Miss Kitty," he drawled. "I intend to find them varmints and lock'em up in the hoose-gow so they'll never trouble you or your loved ones again."

Chapter Two

Caryn should have been angry with Sam's cavalier manner toward her, but how could she be mad at someone who smiled so charmingly even as he patted his pockets for a cigarette while walking out of her office?

"Oh, I forgot one thing," he said, sticking his head back around the door. "I'd like to talk to your staff sometime tomorrow morning."

Caryn consulted her appointment calendar. "I admit I can't speak for the others, so why don't we try for eleven? That hour is usually left pretty free."

Sam nodded. "Fine. See you then."

"Are you sure he knows what he's doing?" Pat asked, ducking inside the office after Sam left.

"If he wasn't reliable, Mr. Gregory certainly wouldn't have promoted him to head up the West Coast security office. I understand he's the golden boy of security," Caryn replied. "Would you please send out a memo stating we're having a staff meeting tomorrow at eleven? Mr. Russell wants to talk to everyone, and we need to do it as soon as possible in hopes of getting this solved."

"I'll get on it right away." Pat made a note in the steno book she carried. "You know, Mr. Russell reminds me of Peter Falk who used to play Columbo, except this man is a lot cuter."

Caryn groaned. "Oh, Pat, now I know I've been working you too hard. The man drinks coffee by the gallon, smokes, probably doesn't know what proper eating habits are, and ten to one his idea of exercise is walking to his car."

"Caryn, my love, there is more to life than aerobics three times a week and eating a balanced diet," Pat reprimanded, "not to mention there is more to life than this magazine. While you're the best example of a person with good eating habits, a major part of the population doesn't live that way. My lunch today consisted of a cheeseburger, french fries and a hot fudge sundae for dessert. Admittedly dinner tonight will be a salad to make up for it, but I don't feel guilty one little bit for pigging out, because I enjoyed every sinful bite."

Caryn smiled. "I wouldn't expect you to. Especially not if you enjoyed yourself. I indulge every once in a while, too."

Pat's eyebrows lifted, her expression one of disbelief as she looked over Caryn's slim figure. "If you indulge it never shows, and I hate people who can get away with it. Unless of course, you're talking about the male species and not junk food."

Caryn sighed, recognizing the beginning of an old argument between them. "You know very well what I mean."

Pat challenged her. "Can you honestly tell me the last time you had a date?"

She stiffened. "I had dinner with Ryan Kincaid a couple of weeks ago."

"That was business. I'm not talking about having dinner with a sexy man whose only interest is work. I'm talking about a man who looks forward to dessert, and I don't mean chocolate mousse, either." Pat paused. "Ah, I'm right. You can't give me an answer, can you?"

Caryn leaned back in her chair, twirling a pencil between her fingers. "If you weren't such a good secretary, along with being a friend, I'd pull rank on you for delving into my private life."

"Give it a rest, Caryn. You have no private life. You go to exercise or ballet class after work on nights you're not staying here late. Or you take your work home with you. You're too young for that kind of life."

Caryn visibly withdrew, the way she did every time someone commented on the way she chose to lead her life. "I'm very happy with my life as it is. Or doesn't that count for anything?"

Pat sighed. "All right, I get the message. I'm coming on like your mother. Just take it from someone who will never see thirty-five again. You can't allow your work to rule you. Oh, by the way, you don't happen to know how old Sam Russell is, do you?"

Caryn couldn't help laughing. "No, but I'd hazard a guess he's in his early thirties, so if you have the courage you can ask him tomorrow. I have an idea he'll give you an honest answer."

"Ten to one he's younger than me, but younger men are in vogue these days, and since all the men my age are chasing twenty-year-olds I have to look at other age groups. To be safe I'll observe him a bit more before I make my move."

Caryn leaned back in her chair. "What happened to that chiropractor you were dating?"

Pat pretended to gag. "He started to talk about going away for some kind of weekend where you find yourself. Of course I was expected to pay my own way, and for that amount of money I could have a great weekend in Hawaii. Since I already know where I am, I suggested he try to do just that and not to bother letting me know when he does find himself. As I always say, the market of available men is very depressing."

"Now you know why I stick with the magazine," Caryn teased, turning away when her telephone rang. She picked it up, said her name and partially turned to say something to Pat when the loud sound of a horn blowing came through the receiver. Her eyes widened as she stared at her secretary. She quickly hung up and rested her trembling hands on top of her desk, lacing the fingers together. "Please call downstairs to see if Mr. Russell has left. If he hasn't, have them send him back up here. Otherwise he might be upstairs in his new office. I want him here as soon as possible."

"Right," Pat breathed, her face pale. "My God, Caryn, if you'd had that phone to your ear you could have gone deaf from that horrible noise." She hurried out to her desk and picked up her own phone, holding it gingerly and a good distance from her own ear.

Caryn sat there, breathing deeply, ordering herself to calm down, which turned out to be easier said than done. She flipped on the intercom. "Pat, find out if

Lori recognized the voice of the person calling and what name was given."

"Gotcha."

Sam walked into Caryn's office fifteen minutes later. He took one look at her pale features and wide eyes and hustled her out of her chair and out of the office, barely giving her time to grab her coat and purse.

"We're having our talk away from the office," he brusquely informed Pat, pausing by the secretary's desk. "Where's the nearest bar?"

She looked wide-eyed. "Brennan's. When you walk out of the building, go left two blocks."

"I am not going anywhere," Caryn informed him in her iciest tone. "I have obligations and appointments this afternoon."

He looked at her. "You have an obligation to yourself first. What just happened has obviously upset you, as it would anyone, we're getting out of here where we can talk in a neutral atmosphere." He took Caryn's arm and practically dragged her out toward the elevator.

"What exactly is wrong with discussing this in my office?" she demanded once the elevator door closed behind them. "After all, don't you want to examine the phone or something?" she asked snidely.

"Walls have ears," he said cryptically. "The phone I want to know about is the one used to make the call, and right now I'm out of luck there. I'm afraid your phone had nothing to do with this episode."

Sam found the bar easily and led Caryn inside. Since it was well before Happy Hour the bar was virtually empty. Sam chose a rear table that afforded them plenty of privacy. A waitress approached them immediately. He ordered a draft beer while Caryn asked for a Perrier with a twist of lime.

He leaned back in his chair, a forefinger rubbing reflectively across his lips. "I want to hear exactly what happened back there."

"Nothing that could leave any clues. The phone rang, I picked it up, said my name and someone set off an air horn," Caryn recited dispassionately. She had calmed herself in the time since it happened.

"Did the person say anything at all before the air horn went off?"

She shook her head. "Not a word. The only thing that saved my hearing was the fact I had partially turned away to say something to Pat. I had Pat question Lori about the caller to find out what he had said to her. All she could tell us was that it was a man and he said he was my father."

Sam frowned. "It has to be someone who either knows you or knows about you."

"What makes you say that?"

"Obviously your father is alive and this person somehow knew it. And if your father was dead, your receptionist would probably know it and question the man further, considering what's been going on lately."

Caryn blinked, impressed with his solid deductions. "You're right. Lori would have questioned anything out of line. Believe me, she has always been very conscientious about her work."

Sam grinned wryly. "I'm well aware of it." He raked his hand through his hair. "Is Lori pretty good at recognizing voices after she's heard them a few times?"

"Excellent at it, which makes her invaluable in her job." Caryn looked up and gave the waitress a smile as she set her glass of Perrier before her. "Once she's heard a voice a few times she recognizes it from then on and she's never been wrong. It's more personal when she greets them by name."

He nodded as he picked up the glass and sipped the foaming brew. "Yet she doesn't know your father's voice?"

Caryn shook her head. "My father wouldn't call me at the office unless it was an emergency. He believes very strongly in keeping work separate from personal life."

Sam shrugged, wishing something, anything, would surface. Especially when an unknown person had tried to destroy Caryn's hearing with a malicious trick, which he didn't think was funny. He felt more frustrated by the minute.

"Files switched around until no one knows where they are, kids' play slime smeared all over file drawers, toy spiders hidden everywhere," he muttered. "Nothing makes sense. They started out as practical jokes that could be found in any office and could be blamed on anyone. Pretty soon they escalate into not so funny jokes and then they start to get dangerous. I hate to warn you, but now is the time to start worrying."

Caryn leaned forward, resting her arms on the table. "Are you saying if the person isn't found soon we could be in some kind of danger? That someone could get hurt before this is all over?" Her eyes grew large with alarm.

"I'm saying it could be a distinct possibility," he replied. "This person is not kidding around, Caryn. I've gone over everything and I can't find a pattern to the destruction. What I'm saying is this stuff isn't happening only on Thursdays or the second Monday of the month or when the moon is full. There's not even a pattern among your staff as victims. They've all been hit and not even in alphabetical order or by seniority. Whoever this guy is he's clever, because he's deliberately not setting a pattern for us to figure out and eventually catch him.''

Caryn smiled. ''Couldn't a woman be just as clever?''

He bowed as elaborately as he could from a sitting position. ''You've made your point. So, have you fooled around with any married guys that would cause an angry wife to set off an air horn over the phone?''

''Married men aren't my style.''

Deciding it would be prudent not to pursue that topic any further, Sam finished his beer, asked if Caryn wanted another Perrier and gestured to the waitress for another round.

''Aren't you going to tap the phones or set a trap or something?'' Caryn demanded. ''We can't afford to live in this kind of fear. I'm certainly going to be more cautious when I answer the phone from now on.''

''Only in the movies when the inspector has a clue no one knows about can you set a trap. One thing I would like to do is get everyone's fingerprints, and dust for prints the next time something happens in the office. It may be a waste of time, but then again, we may come up with something.''

''No one is going to like that,'' she warned. ''They're going to feel as if one of them is the criminal and I can't blame them. I'd feel that way, too.''

''Maybe they will, but I can't allow anyone's tender feelings to get in the way. If I'm going to get the job done I have to try everything I can.'' He leaned back and smiled when the waitress set his drink in front of him. "Look, I know none of this is easy."

"Do you? We come in the mornings not sure what we'll find. Everyone is afraid to come in by themselves, even me. I feel nervous when I stay late and the janitor is usually within calling distance, since I generally don't stay after he cleans our offices. How can you know how that feels?" She wasn't sure if she was feeling frustrated or irritated at what she thought was a lack of progress in the case.

"Caryn, your office isn't the only one to have something like this happen to you," Sam told her. "Wes Com's computer division in Atlanta had a very similar problem, except their programs were screwed up and some unique messages and occasionally obscene ones would suddenly appear on computer screens. A few of the employees were left pretty upset from everything—one was ready for a nervous breakdown. It turned out to be a teenage hacker who had broken into the system and was having a high old time until he was caught. He created more havoc in a short period of time than a team of professionals could. One of my people who's trained in computer theft finally tracked him down."

"Computers I could understand someone going after, but the offices for a fitness magazine doesn't make any sense," Caryn argued, squeezing her wedge of lime into her drink. "We're not a threat to anyone."

"To be honest I can't see it, either, but there's some pretty strange people in this world," he admitted. "Believe me, I've met more than my share of them."

"What got you into this kind of work?" she asked curiously.

"I wanted to be a cop, but I hate uniforms, so this seemed the next best thing for me. In school, a few instructors said I'd make a pretty good private investigator because I tend to dance to my own tune and come to conclusions my own way without going through the proper channels."

"You don't like to be part of the system," Caryn guessed correctly.

He pointed his forefinger at her and cocked his thumb. "You got it."

She chuckled. "My secretary views you as sort of a Columbo. It appears she isn't all that wrong."

He grimaced, picturing television's rumpled police detective. "I wouldn't be caught dead in a raincoat, not to mention that heap he called a car."

Caryn looked around, just then realizing the noise level in the bar had risen greatly as had the number of occupants. Happy Hour was well on its way, and the singles were eager to make new friends. She quickly finished her drink and reached for her coat and purse.

"It appears our time of peace and quiet has come to an end." She smiled at Sam. "Thanks for the drinks. I only wish I had more information for you. I don't feel I gave you much help."

He grinned. "Don't worry about it. That would make the job too easy. I like a challenge."

They walked outside and back toward the office building.

"I'm having my car shipped out," Sam said, "and hopefully it will be arriving within the week. I also have to find a place to live that's convenient to the office. I'm not all that fond of hotel rooms, probably because I've been in them so much for the past five years. After a while, they tend to look alike. Although, considering the suite I got this time, I could make an exception.''

''Finding a place to live close by is next to impossible,'' Caryn told him, tucking her hands in the warm confines of her coat pockets. ''I live about a half hour away and consider myself lucky. It's a fairly new complex, so I got lucky when I found my place.''

''Apartment?''

''Town house.''

Sam looked interested. ''If I can't find anything would you mind if I took a look over there? I'm considered a fairly decent neighbor. Probably because I'm not home very much. In fact, if you like I'll try to find something the farthest distance from you, okay?''

Caryn stood back a few paces and studied him. ''My idea of a decent neighbor is one who doesn't borrow everything and doesn't play the stereo at all hours of the night. I do a lot of paperwork at home, where I don't have to worry about interruptions.''

Sam understood her meaning, loud and clear. If he wanted to move into her complex, fine, but that didn't mean he would be invited over for dinner twice a week. He wondered if it would help if he told her what a lousy cook he was, which was the truth. Then he looked over at her. Maybe she wasn't all that great at cooking, either.

''I just want to find a place to live,'' he assured her. ''I tend to keep to myself and I wear headphones when I play my stereo.''

Caryn's lips twitched. ''I find that hard to believe.''

''I also don't hold wild parties or run naked through the grounds.''

"Your future neighbors will be relieved to hear that."

"When I do have a party I invite everyone in the immediate area. It cuts down on complaints." They stepped inside the lobby, Caryn with the intention of taking the elevator down to the underground parking garage and Sam to call a cab.

"If you'd like I can drop you off at your hotel," she offered, as she punched the elevator call button.

"Thanks, but I can take a cab."

"It's no problem," she assured him.

Sam hung up the phone and walked toward her. "I never turn down that kind of offer."

They soon reached the garage, and Caryn led him toward a charcoal gray Porsche parked in a reserved spot.

"To tell you the truth I expected you to drive a BMW," he confided, sliding into the passenger seat.

She slanted an amused look at him. "Then this must have been quite a shock for you." She pushed in the clutch and put the car in gear.

"I could live with it." Sam quickly changed his mind as they roared out onto the boulevard. "Did you forget to tell me something? Such as that you're in training for the Grand Prix?" he asked, one hand on the door handle, the other gripping the dash.

She smiled. "I'm just assuring myself a place in the traffic. You can't hesitate around here." She zoomed into the other lane earning a angry motorist's horn and waving hand.

"Assuring, my foot. You're ordering these people to let you in or else." He closed his eyes when she raced through a yellow light. "Please, I'm too young to die. I still have a lot I want to do."

In what seemed like seconds, Caryn pulled up in front of Sam's hotel and waved off the parking valet as she braked to a stop just past the entrance.

"You can relax now."

He looked at her cautiously. "When did we land?"

Caryn half turned in the low-slung seat. "Aren't you ever serious?"

He turned his head. "Sure I am. But I learned a long time ago if you look as if you don't really care or know what you're doing, people tend to get careless and then you move in for the kill. How do you think I solve most of my cases?"

"So it's all an act."

He shrugged. "Is it? Thanks for the supersonic flight. Remind me to check on my life insurance before I travel with you again." He slid out of the car, and with a casual wave of the hand sauntered across the driveway toward the hotel lobby.

Caryn watched him for a moment then sped off. She knew what her unsettling feeling stemmed from. First the phone call that upset her, then spending time with a man who probably didn't know what the word *serious* meant. She could feel the tightening of nerves in her stomach.

She drove through the rush-hour traffic, zipping in and out with casual ease, but her mind was elsewhere.

"What's going to happen next?" she muttered under her breath, turning on the car radio and selecting a station that played golden oldies. "Russell better find out soon." With an abrupt shift of thought processes, she mentally reviewed her refrigerator and kitchen cabinets and decided to stop at the grocery store on her way home.

An hour and a half later, Caryn had put away her groceries and fixed herself a dinner. Dressed in pale blue sweatpants and a dark gold T-shirt, she wandered around the house, nibbling from the plate she carried. Her eyes were blank as she was lost in a world of her own making. After a time she set the plate down and walked out to the attached garage.

She smiled thinly as she released the lock on a freezer. "People probably think I keep a body in here," she murmured, inspecting the contents.

Chapter Three

"You look like you have a hangover," Sam commented, walking up to Caryn when she entered the conference room. "What in the world did you drink after you dropped me off?"

She almost dropped the coffee carafe. "As I rarely drink alcohol that would be next to impossible," she muttered.

Sam's eyes narrowed, noting Caryn's pallid features, trembling hands and jerky motions. "Are you all right? Did that call upset you more than you let on yesterday?"

"I am fine," she replied tartly.

He exhaled. "No, you're not. If anything like this happens again I want you to call me if you feel the least uptight about it, okay?"

Caryn spun around, facing him with a set expression. "I didn't realize you have a psychology degree, also."

"I understand tension that stems from problems like this. I mean it, I want you to call."

Without replying, Caryn walked away. She already knew she didn't look her best. She had worn her favorite bronze suit in hopes that the warm hue would reflect some color to her face, but Pat's concern earlier and Sam's comment now told her she hadn't succeeded. She made a hurried trip back to her office for a quick application of lipstick and blusher.

"You honestly think that's going to make a difference?"

She turned at Sam's skeptical tone. He leaned against the doorway, his arms crossed in front of him.

"Don't you think you should be talking to the staff?" she asked sharply.

"The meeting can't start without the boss."

Caryn took several deep breaths to calm her jangling nerves. "Then we better return to the conference room." She walked toward the doorway. For a moment Sam stared at her, his piercing eyes boring into hers. She stared back, mentally crossing her fingers that he wouldn't try to question her further.

"You still look tired," he said quietly.

"How I look is none of your business," she said deliberately. She moved forward a step, hoping she wouldn't have to brush past him to leave the room. Sam stood there watching her for another minute before slowly moving away. He waited until she passed him, and he walked behind her.

Caryn continued breathing deeply, feeling a roaring sound in her ears. She felt as if Sam was looking deep inside her and she hated him for it.

"Caryn?" Tami stood in the conference-room doorway. "Is everything okay?" She glanced past her boss at the stern-featured man following her.

"I'm fine and I wish everyone would just stop asking me that," Caryn snapped, then quickly lowered her voice. "I'm sorry, Tami. All of this has been very distressing."

She smiled. "I know what you mean."

They entered the large room and sat at the oval table with Caryn gesturing Sam to the head of the table and taking the chair on his left. When coffee was passed around, he took one look at the carafe, made a face and shook his head. Caryn couldn't help smiling as she poured a cup for herself.

"Everyone, this is Sam Russell, the head of the new West Coast security office, which will be housed upstairs," she told them after the group settled down. "Hopefully, he'll be able to solve the mystery of our vandal before we find the office down around our ears," she said lightly.

"If we've written out those lengthy reports, why are we here?" Janna, one of the assistant editors, asked. "They said what's happened to us. Isn't that enough?"

"Not really, because I need as much input from you as possible. You'd be surprised what you might have stored in the back of your mind if someone happens to ask the right questions to trigger those memories," Sam replied, starting to pull a cigarette pack out of his shirt pocket. Then he remembered where he was and the lack of ashtrays on the table. With a wry expression he pushed them back in. "Reports give me dry details. What I want to do is have you talk about your experiences and hope you don't mind if I occasionally interrupt you with questions for clarification." He checked a sheet of paper in front of him. "Why don't we start with Lee. You're the nutrition editor, am I right?"

She nodded. "I write a column and oversee any articles on the subject."

"And you found kids' play slime all over the contents of files when you came in one morning?" He rested his elbows on the tabletop, lacing his fingers together.

Lee grimaced. "That's putting it mildly. To be honest, I came in and found a mess."

"What time did you come in that morning?"

"About eight o'clock, my usual time."

"And what time did you leave the night before?"

She frowned, searching her memory. "I think I stayed late that night because a story needed to be proofed, so I probably left here around six or six-thirty. I'm sorry, I don't know the exact time."

Sam jotted down notes in the margin of the paper in front of him. "Do you remember seeing anything or anyone unusual that night? Strangers walking around in the hall or in the parking garage downstairs?"

Lee chewed on her lower lip as she tried to recall that time. "No, I'm sorry I don't remember anything out of the ordinary. After all, it has been a few weeks, and I don't have the best memory to begin with. I also wasn't looking for anything."

He nodded. "Did anyone else work late that night?"

She shook her head. "It was just me, and the only person I saw was Larry, the janitor. He was vacuuming the reception area when I left."

"And Jay, you came in one morning and found all your negatives scattered around your studio?" Sam turned to the head photographer.

"They weren't just thrown around in my studio. A lot of them were also scratched and others cut into confetti," he said angrily. "More than fifty percent of the negatives were ruined, including a brand-new set I had shot the night before. The cost of a second session didn't help the budget one bit.''

Or make Mr. Gregory happy, Caryn thought to herself, recalling her boss's anger over the increase. She had spent the morning on the phone with him as he demanded to know what progress had been made, and she had to tell him nothing had cropped up yet. He loudly informed her to get on the ball and get the problem taken care of and cooperate with Sam. Eliott Gregory was the best boss around when everything was going fine, but once one of his businesses was being tampered with he turned into the mean old man many people feared.

Sam continued talking to the rest of the staff and jotting down whatever data they gave. He asked questions, pulling information they might not have thought about. As he worked, he absently tugged at his shirt collar. Every once in a while he glanced at Caryn. Each time he saw her she was dressed impeccably, making him feel as if she was in charge instead of him. He fought the urge to fix his tie, except he wasn't wearing one.

''You think this is someone on the inside, don't you?'' Jodi, the editor for hair and fashion, asked. She combed her platinum blond spiky hair with her fingertips, looking as agitated as the others. She laughed. ''Good grief, I sound like a detective in a mystery novel, don't I? But you know what I mean? Someone who works on this floor or has access to this area, which is virtually anyone in this building if they wanted to get in here badly enough.''

"More than anything, I'm trying to look for a motive," he replied. "The best idea I've come up with is revenge."

Revenge? They all looked at him with varied expressions of shock.

"Why would anyone be angry enough at us to exact revenge?" Caryn spoke what the others felt. "We're a fitness magazine, not a corporation dealing with computers or defense contracts. What could any of us have done to cause someone to want retribution?"

"You don't have to be a multimillion-dollar firm to have enemies," he countered. "I read in a newspaper once about a dry cleaner who was bitter rivals with a competitor. Soon paint was splashed on one's front windows. Another found its interior vandalized. I understand the magazine reviews the pros and cons of various diet plans, exercise equipment and so on."

"That's right," Caryn replied. "Are you trying to say someone we panned could be doing all this?"

"It's not a new story." He slid his notes into a manila folder. "I'd like a list of companies you've written about in the past year."

"That could be a pretty long list," Caryn muttered, watching Pat write down Sam's suggestion.

"She's right, it will take some time even with the computer," the secretary said. "We don't list our files by the ones we've discussed negatively."

"Would it be possible to get me even a few names and addresses by morning?"

"That I can do. I'll look for the most recent."

"I thank you for coming at such short notice." Sam flashed them a warm smile. "I know this hasn't been easy for you and, unfortunately, may get rougher before we get this settled. But I intend to get to the bottom of this."

"I think we'll all say amen to that." Jodi chuckled, rising from her chair. "I don't know about the rest of you, but I'm ready for lunch."

Sam lightly grasped Caryn's arm, keeping her beside him. "I have to put a call in to Mr. Gregory this afternoon for an update on the situation," he murmured. "I thought you might like to be present during the call."

She grimaced, looking as if she was preparing herself for a spoonful of nasty-tasting medicine. "I'll be honest with you. I wouldn't like to be present, but I guess I should be."

Sam nodded. "I'm afraid so. Why don't you come up a little before three."

"All right. You know, most corporation heads have their underlings take these kind of reports. This is one time when I wish he wasn't so heavily involved in the day-to-day running of all his concerns."

Sam understood only too well. Eliott Gregory was a man well-known for putting his nose in where it wasn't appreciated or needed. Sam had more than his share of run-ins with the irascible man in past years and knew there would be more in the future.

"I warned him in the beginning this might not be easy," Sam explained.

"But we both know patience has never been one of his virtues."

"Funny, I didn't know he had any virtues." He glanced at his watch. "I've got a luncheon meeting with a couple of prospective investigators for this office. I'll see you at three, then?"

She nodded. "I'll be there."

Sam placed his hand on her shoulder. "Cheer up, he can't bite over the phone. See you later."

Left alone in the conference room, Caryn sat back down and rested her face in her hands. She could feel the pressure moving in from all directions, and she wondered what it would take to get it to stop. A few minutes later, she came up with her own conclusion.

AT TEN TO THREE Caryn entered Sam's suite of offices, situated four floors above hers. The receptionist, who could have doubled for a magazine centerfold, smiled at Caryn and buzzed Sam.

"Hi. Care for a quick grand tour?" he asked, greeting her with a warm handshake.

"Why not?" She smiled back, looking around at the earth-tone decor. "Very masculine looking. Don't the women working for you object?"

"I had nothing to do with the decor," he admitted. "I have two female investigators, and I told them they could do anything they wanted with their office. They share one since they're on the road so much." He opened a door and indicated a small office with cream walls and bright-colored art-gallery posters. "For the time being, space is at a premium in here. Luckily with everyone in and out so much no one minds sharing."

"Why do you have so many investigators? I guess what I'm asking is what exactly do you do?" Caryn entered toward an end office Sam indicated.

"The investigators visit the various holdings for security spot checks," he explained. "Mr. Gregory has very definite ideas on what security measures are to be used, and these spot checks insure that they are. Also, if there is a security problem we go in and evaluate the problem and hopefully solve it."

"Have you ever been stumped?" She took a seat near his desk, glancing at the butt-filled ashtray.

He reddened. "Just once, and it's a time I wish I could forget, although it was a good lesson. The alarm system in a shopping mall Wes Com owned was going off for no apparent reason, calling the police out at all hours of the night, and our own security people were going crazy. They couldn't understand what was going on because there was never a sign of forced entry. We went through three alarm systems before I decided to spend the night there along with a few remote cameras."

"And?"

Sam sighed. "To this day I don't know exactly how it all happened. It appeared a cat was sneaking through a hole in the wall in hopes of finding food and tripped the main alarm each time she got in."

Caryn burst out laughing. "Now that's what I call a cat burglar."

"No kidding. One of the shop owners insisted on adopting the cat so she wouldn't be sent to the animal shelter and called her Robbie after Cary Grant's character in *To Catch a Thief*," he said, flipping through his Rolodex. "You ready to talk to The Man?"

"No."

He cast her a sympathetic smile. "C'mon, the sooner we do this, the sooner it's over with." He picked up his phone and punched out the number of the head office in New York. It was after office hours, but he knew the boss would be there waiting for his call. The line was picked up before the first ring barely ended. The moment the call was connected, Sam punched the button activating the speaker phone.

"Gregory here," a raspy voice barked, startling Caryn by its abrupt tone.

"It's Sam Russell, Mr. Gregory."

"You're two minutes late calling in, Russell. What have you learned so far?"

Sam grimaced. "There was another incident yesterday. This one to Ms. Richards. Someone called in and asked for her and when she picked up the phone the jerk set of an air horn over the line. I'm sure you're aware what kind of damage that could have caused her ear."

"Is she all right?"

Sam looked at Caryn.

"I'm fine, Mr. Gregory," she spoke up. "Luckily I had turned away at the last moment and didn't receive the sound full force."

"I want to know who's trying to screw with my magazine." His voice boomed over the line. "When you find the person I want him strung up by his heels. And I want it taken care of soon, do you hear me? This shouldn't have happened in the first place."

"You of all people know this kind of problem isn't solved overnight," Sam interjected. "I honestly feel the motive here is revenge and I plan to check into it further, but you have to remember I'm also setting up a new office here and that takes time."

"Time *I'm* paying for. I want *Simple Fitness* brought back on track or I'll send someone out there who can do it," he ordered. "As for you, Caryn, you just keep doing the job you're paid for." With that the line was abruptly disconnected.

"The man has a heart of gold," Caryn said dryly. "I'm sure he's more upset over the magazine than the staff's physical and mental health."

"He's more talk than anything."

"Not where I'm concerned." Caryn could feel the pressure building up again. And here she thought she had taken care of it. "Some of the board members weren't too pleased at the idea of someone my age taking on the position of editor-in-chief, and I'm sure they're coming out with I-told-you-so's. I've had to do the work of ten people to prove them wrong and make sure not to step out of line once. I worked seven days a week to bring the magazine up to where it is today, and if I don't keep up the pace I could lose it all. And no vandal is going to take this away from me," she said fiercely, leaning forward in her chair.

Sam watched her tense posture and amber eyes glittering with purpose. At the moment Caryn looked ready to do battle with the devil himself if it meant keeping the magazine together.

"Gregory was wrong," he said quietly. "That magazine isn't his. It's yours from top to bottom. And I intend to find the person behind all this. But I'm not doing this for him. I'm doing this for you."

She sat back, startled by his words. "Why would you do it for me?"

He shrugged. "Maybe because I prefer working for a beautiful woman instead of a crusty old man who smokes smelly cigars and thinks he's God."

Caryn opened her mouth to say something, then just as quickly closed it again. All she knew was that the pressure was building up again, probably because of listening to Mr. Gregory's not so subtle threats. She pushed herself out of her chair.

"I have to get back," she said abruptly. Without looking at him, she hurried out of his office.

Sam frowned at her sudden withdrawal. He waited fifteen minutes, then punched out a few numbers.

"Yes, Sam Russell calling for Caryn Richards," he said crisply.

"I'm sorry, Mr. Russell," Lori said in her superefficient voice, "but Ms. Richards isn't taking any calls. Would you care to speak to her secretary?"

"I'm sure she'll speak to me." Sam injected a bit of arrogance in his voice.

Lori's hesitation was evident over the phone. "She said especially you, Mr. Russell."

Sam quietly replaced the receiver without saying a word. He stared long and hard at the phone, picturing Caryn's face when she left his office.

"Coward."

Chapter Four

"What do you think you're doing?" Caryn stood in the doorway, dressed in a sweat-soaked T-shirt and sweatpants, her hair pulled back in a casual ponytail, and no makeup.

She looked a far cry from the impeccably dressed woman he saw during the workweek. He decided he liked her better this way.

"Hi there, it's Saturday morning and I'm new in town," he explained. "I thought you might take pity on me and be willing to take in some of the sights." He held up a paper bag. "I even brought doughnuts."

Caryn hesitated. "I have some paperwork I intended to do today."

"No housecleaning?"

"It's easier to have someone come in to do that." She held the door open wider and gestured with her hand. "Come on in."

Sam glanced down at his watch. It was barely eight o'clock. "You start your days early, don't you? Or don't you realize it's Saturday and you're allowed to sleep late?"

"It appears you were up early, too." Caryn led the way back to the kitchen where she had been making a pot of coffee when the doorbell rang.

During their trek to the kitchen Sam's keen eyes noticed one thing—for a woman who wore strong colors in the workplace, her home was the picture of serenity with a pastel color scheme.

Caryn opened a white-painted cabinet and pulled out two coffee mugs. "The coffee is safe," she assured him. "You will definitely have your caffeine fix."

He raised an eyebrow. "This from the woman who talks about caffeine stimulating hunger and how it isn't good for you?"

"I would say just about all of us drink regular coffee when at home. I'm sure we would be considered hypocrites, but no one's perfect." She filled the two mugs and carried them over to a small ice-cream table set in a breakfast nook. "Is it going to upset you if I mention I don't have an ashtray in the house?"

He shook his head. "No, I don't have to have a cigarette every hour on the hour."

Sam looked around at the wallpaper of violets on two walls, and the lavender and pale green color scheme carried on the plates, place mats and towels. "Very nice," he commented. "It must be a soothing haven for you when you've had a rough day at work."

Her head snapped up, the look on her face one of shock that a virtual stranger could so easily guess one of her secrets.

"I never could understand why a builder would choose this color scheme for a kitchen," she mumbled, burying her nose in the fragrant steam coming from her mug.

Sam knew better, but he wasn't going to say anything. Instead, he opened the white bag and pulled out a chocolate-frosted doughnut, placing it in front of him, and a plain cake doughnut, putting it in front of Caryn.

"I asked. The calorie content is very low," he assured her, as he bit into his doughnut.

She chuckled as she tore off a small piece and brought it to her lips. "You're a very pushy man, Sam Russell."

"It's part of the job."

She froze. "Is that why you're here? Has something else happened?"

He shook his head. "No, today I'm off duty. I'm here because I want to go sight-seeing and I don't like to go alone."

"Why me? I have a staff of lovely women who would jump at the chance of showing you around," she told him.

Sam hooked an arm around the back of his chair. "They already know how to have fun. I don't think you do."

She stiffened. "My private life is the way I like it."

He held up his hands in surrender. "Don't get your back up. As I said, all I want is some company while I look around for a place to live and get to know the area. Please?"

She hesitated as she systematically tore the doughnut into small pieces and ate it that way. "And if I refuse?"

"Then I'll just sit here, drink all your coffee and eat my doughnuts. In general, make a nuisance of myself." He smiled with great charm.

Caryn nodded. "Somehow I thought you'd say that," she said wryly, standing up. "All right. Help yourself to more coffee while I shower and change." She walked out of the kitchen and climbed the stairs.

While refilling his cup Sam took a quick peek at the downstairs area, which consisted of a small formal dining area, living room and bathroom. He discovered a door in the kitchen opened onto a set of stairs leading downward to a garage. He glanced at another set of stairs that led to a loft area, and he could see the beginning of a hallway that must have led to the bedrooms.

"Very nice," he murmured, returning to the table and another doughnut.

Within a half hour, Caryn returned downstairs, now dressed in faded jeans and a soft coral pullover sweater that stopped before the waistband of her jeans. Tan loafers finished her outfit. Her damp hair was pulled back in a French braid. Sam noticed even her makeup was more subdued than what she wore in the office. He also noticed this woman appeared much more approachable than the one he'd first met several days before.

"Very nice," he complimented her.

"I couldn't let you outshine me." She gestured toward his jeans, aged by time, and a forest-green wool crewneck. She opened the hall closet and withdrew a brown leather bomber jacket.

"I unplugged your coffeepot and rinsed out the pot," he told her as she turned to go into the kitchen.

"Thank you."

They walked outside and headed for the visitors parking lot at one end of the complex, where a rec center and swimming pool were.

"This is really nice." Sam looked around the condos, which were built to look like tiny ranch houses, nestled among trees and grassy areas, with streams running between each section of four condos. "I can see why you like it. It's not only fairly close to your office but it has a homey feeling instead of the sterile exterior you see in so many complexes."

"The occupants are either single, or couples with no children," Caryn explained, shrugging on her jacket against the morning chill. "The units have one or two bedrooms, depending on what your requirements are."

"What about a loft, such as what you have?"

She nodded. "Only the one bedroom units have a loft. I use it as an office. It works out well for me."

Sam took her arm leading her toward a Mustang convertible that had to be twenty years old, judging by the body style. "My baby arrived yesterday," he said with a note of pride, unlocking and opening the passenger door. "I washed and waxed her first thing this morning."

"You were too young to drive when this car was built," she commented, sliding onto the leather bucket seat.

His face momentarily clouded. "It was my brother's. He bought her brand new and always kept her in excellent shape, because he said these cars would become classics some day."

"Then I'm surprised he didn't keep it." The moment Sam started up the engine, Caryn knew she was sitting in a car that was almost as powerful as her Porsche. And from the purr under the hood she knew it had been faithfully kept up.

"He died eight years ago. His widow said she knew he would want me to have the car." He put the car in reverse and carefully backed out of the parking space.

Caryn looked at his profile, noting the lines bracketing from his mouth and realized he wasn't as carefree as he liked the world to think he was.

"I'm sure he would be glad to know someone is taking such excellent care of it," she said softly, feeling the need to give him comfort.

He momentarily turned his head an smiled. "Yeah, he would probably tell me I use the brakes too much and I can't shift worth a damn. You know what? I wouldn't mind hearing him yell at me one more time."

Caryn thought of asking how his brother died, then quickly changed her mind. She doubted it was a subject Sam wanted to discuss just yet.

"I circled some ads in the newspaper," he said, using his thumb to point behind him. "They're in the backseat. Would you mind looking through them and telling me which ones are good and which ones aren't? You know the area better than I do."

She leaned over her seat and pulled the paper toward her. "We should have done this at my place," she told him, gazing over the ads circled with a green felt-tip pen. She withdrew a pen from her purse and carefully crossed out the ads she felt were unsuitable and put check marks by the ones she felt would be better for his needs, while he explained what he wanted.

"I really want something with an attached enclosed garage, which is another reason I don't want an apartment," he explained. "And a fairly reasonable commute. What you have isn't too bad."

"Some of the older apartment houses have enclosed garages, but they are hard to find," she replied. "A few of these aren't as close as you'd like, but you still might like to check them out. We should have made some calls from my house to make sure these places are still available."

"I called on them last night after I picked up the paper." Sam pulled over to the curb to double-check his city map.

"This one first," Caryn suggested. "It's not all that far from here and in a nice area."

Sam's optimism quickly flew out the window as they went from one ad to another. Everywhere they went he found fault with the place.

"There was nothing wrong with that town house," Caryn argued, after they left their fourth choice. "It had the garage you wanted, plenty of room inside, the rent was certainly reasonable, and the kitchen appliances were included."

"And the next-door neighbor had two small dogs that did nothing but bark while we were there," he grumbled. "I didn't know dogs that small could make so much noise. No thanks. Now where do we go?"

She consulted the newspaper. "A two-bedroom, one-bath rental with a yard," she read. "Turn left at the next light. Tell me, what did you have in Chicago?"

Sam grimaced. "An apartment on the fourteenth floor, underground parking and a rent that rivaled the national debt. It was very high tech with white walls and a space-age kitchen. This time around I want something with personality. I wasn't in my other place long enough at one time to hate it, so it didn't matter. There, I didn't have room to work on my car. Either I drove out to my parents' and used their garage, or I paid a mechanic to do what I could easily handle for a lot less money.''

At first glance the small bungalow appeared perfect for Sam's needs. A roomy garage was in the rear, no small yapping dogs next door. The commuting distance to work was a bit more than Sam might have liked, but he said he could live with it. Caryn had offered to check out the closets and kitchen to make sure everything looked all right, while he inspected the rest of the place. Just as she was opening kitchen cabinets to see how much room they had, she heard sounds in the rear bathroom that didn't sound promising. She glanced inside the large cabinet, groaned at the ants scattering and quickly closed the doors. Walking back to where Sam was she found him with the landlord unsuccessfully trying to stop a flood of water coming from the commode.

"I would suggest you call a plumber," Sam commented.

"Plumbers cost too much. I've got a friend who can fix it in no time." Since the man didn't appear to know what he was doing, Sam finally shut off the water leading to the tank. "So, you want the place?" the man asked hopefully. "You can move in today."

Sam looked at Caryn who rolled her eyes. "I don't think so."

"What did you do?" she demanded to know once they returned to his car.

"Nothing much. I just flushed the toilet. I wanted to see if it was in working order. Ironically, just as I was doing it the landlord got this strange look on his face." He chuckled. "I think he knew there was a problem with the plumbing. What did you find?"

Caryn shuddered. "Ants. I hate them with a passion. It seems once you've had them they're almost impossible to get rid of, unless you're on top of the problem constantly. Too bad, because the kitchen seemed very nice and had a lot of cabinet space."

"Probably a good thing you didn't turn on the faucet or we could have had a flood." Sam glanced at his watch. "It's almost one. How about lunch?"

Caryn looked out the window. "I'm not really all that hungry."

"You must be. Come on, pick a place."

She hesitated. "There is a nice place that serves all sorts of different kinds of soups and salads."

"Don't you believe in hamburgers?" He sighed. "Okay, where is it?"

Caryn directed him to the homey-looking restaurant. Sam looked relieved to see the soup servings were large and patrons could get seconds at no extra charge. He chose the cheese soup and a large salad, then two huge blueberry muffins to go with it, while Caryn fixed herself a smaller salad.

"No wonder you're so thin. You hardly eat anything," he grumbled, as they found a table in the crowded restaurant. "Why don't you take part of my muffin?"

"This is plenty for me, honest," she assured him. "A heavy meal in the middle of the day makes me sleepy, so I tend to eat light then."

"Makes sense. Some days when I've overdone it at lunch I'm more than ready for a nap." Sam liberally buttered a muffin.

"It's already obvious you eat anything put in front of you. What kind of exercise do you do to keep your weight down?'' Caryn asked, watching him demolish half the muffin in no time.

"Running is boring. The few times I've looked over those health clubs I see nothing more than Barbie and Ken dolls dressed up to work out and make new friends, and I find tennis boring,'' he told her. "I play a mean game of golf and I swim if I'm in the mood. So I guess I would say I have no set exercise program. As for weight, none of my family has a weight problem and they eat pretty much what they want. Oh, I admit I don't pig out in the middle of the night with a gigantic hot fudge sundae or eat half a cake, but I don't believe in giving up what tastes good just because some people say it's bad for you. This is really good.'' Sam continued dipping his spoon into the thick soup. "Now that you know I'm not into any healthy activities, why don't you tell me what got you interested in working for a fitness magazine?''

Caryn toyed with her salad. "My father is a college football coach. I have one brother who's a doctor specializing in sports medicine, and my other brother is a college baseball coach. I was on the girl's track team in high school and college, and I've always enjoyed running. I feel it clears my head. Then I discovered creative writing in high school and learned I had a talent for it, so I decided to combine the two. Going to work for *Simple Fitness* was the next logical step.''

"True,'' Sam said. "I think I'll get another helping of soup. Do you want anything?''

She smiled and shook her head. "I am going to ask for more iced tea. Would you like another glass?''

"Yes, thanks.''

This time Sam chose corn muffins to go with his soup and plopped one in front of Caryn. "C'mon, try one. You're too skinny as it is," he informed her.

"Not when I'm photographed," she argued. "The camera puts a good ten to fifteen pounds on a person." But to please him she took a small bite of the corn muffin and pronounced it very good.

"We've pretty well run out of places to look at." He sighed. "I don't know whether to buy another paper or try one of those rental agencies."

"Neither," Caryn told him after a slight pause, while she looked as if she was trying to make up her mind. "There's several units for rent in my complex and I know the owner of two of them. We can call him from my place and see if they're still available."

Sam looked at her long and hard. "Naturally you knew about these places when I came by this morning and when I kidded you before about moving in there."

She nodded.

"Was I expected to pass some test before you brought this up, and if I hadn't passed would you have kept quiet about it?"

Caryn realized Sam wasn't angry as much as he was hurt. "Some years ago I suggested to a coworker that he try a unit two doors from mine that I knew was available. The problem was he thought I was suggesting a closer relationship between us. It got more than a little sticky before it was straightened out."

Sam nodded, now understanding her need for caution. "And because there were times you thought I was coming on to you when I was merely being my old friendly self, you could see the same thing happening all over again if you didn't nip it in the bud, right?"

She nodded. "As I said, it got a bit complicated and I don't intend to go through that kind of situation again."

"Then I'm surprised you were willing to come out with me today, unless you were hoping you could talk me into another place." His eyes narrowed. "Caryn, did he ever try to hurt you?"

She smiled sadly. "Only with words, and as we both know there are times they can hurt just as much as physical violence. Needless to say when I was promoted, he took another position." She held up her hand to stem the words she knew he would speak. "Before you get any wild ideas about his being the person you're looking for, I think I should tell you he took a job out of state that carried a promotion and an excellent pay raise. He had no reason to get back at me or the magazine."

Sam finished his soup in silence. He'd discovered he was learning a lot more about Caryn than he'd expected. He freely admitted he wouldn't have been surprised if she had worn a business suit while they went apartment hunting. Today she seemed much freer, more relaxed about herself and the world around her. But he'd still hazard a guess that she had no idea how to have real fun, and he was determined to change that as soon as possible.

"Ready?"

"One quick stop." Caryn picked up her purse as he picked up the bill.

"I'll wait for you out in the parking lot." Sam left the tip and walked toward the front of the restaurant. He dug a pack of cigarettes and his lighter out of his shirt pocket and lit up, drawing the smoke deep into his lungs. Out of consideration for Caryn he hadn't smoked in the car and now felt he needed a cigarette. He leaned against the front fender of the car, idly looking around the parking lot, which was part of a large shopping mall.

"You must have been dying for that." Caryn walked up to stand in front of him.

"Desperate maybe." He used the hand holding his cigarette to gesture toward the mall. "When I do find a place I'll have to hustle out and get some furniture."

"What about the furniture you have in your old apartment?"

Sam shook his head. "I rented the furniture along with the apartment. It was easier that way. My mom packed up my linens, clothing and my personal items. She's holding them until I send for them. And living in a hotel isn't all it's cracked up to be, even with maid and room service."

"Then let's get back to my place and make that call," Caryn suggested. "I hate the idea of you being imprisoned in a luxury hotel more than you have to be."

"You probably think I'm nuts to want to give up a hotel suite. But then you don't have to use their towels," he grumbled, opening the door for her. "I don't think they know what fabric softener is. They're also not very large."

The moment they returned to Caryn's condo she leafed through her address book and found the number she was looking for. She placed the call, and Sam was able to look at both condos within a half hour. One, which ironically was across from Caryn, was available immediately. Sam wasted no time in writing out a check for the man who was to be his landlord.

"I guess I wasted your day running around," he apologized.

"Actually I had fun," she admitted honestly, surprised by her admission. "Sometimes it's interesting to see what other places look like."

Sam smiled. "So did I. And if I hope to move in as soon as possible I better get out and buy myself a bed and a few other important items."

"Such as a coffee maker and coffee?" she asked dryly.

"You better be careful, Caryn, or people will think you have a sense of humor." He stopped before he walked out the door. "Caryn, I'd like to be your friend. No strings attached. Just someone you can call on if you have a problem, okay?"

She couldn't help smiling back. "All right. Just one thing..."

He was busy pulling his cigarette pack and lighter out of his pocket. "What's that?"

"I don't care how good a friend you think you're going to be, you still can't smoke in my house."

Chapter Five

"The next time Jack has a cousin in town and you need a last-minute blind date, do not call me," Tami told Lee as they walked into Caryn's office.

"Tami, I swear I didn't know!" she protested. "Jack told me he was a great guy."

"And Jack also admitted he hadn't seen him since they were ten." Tami turned to Caryn. "This man was unbelievable. He wanted to visit every topless bar in the county. We won't even discuss his clothing and so-called eating habits."

Caryn turned to Lee. "That bad?"

She grimaced. "Worse. I told Jack he owes us a very expensive dinner and a dozen roses each for putting up with good old Harry. So, how was your weekend?"

Caryn shrugged. "Quiet." To her way of thinking that was an understatement. She had spent Sunday afternoon looking out her kitchen window watching Sam move a few boxes into the condo across from hers and dragging large shopping bags inside. Not once did he look her way or even come by. She told herself she should be grateful he wasn't going to be a nuisance, but she knew she was lying. She handed an interoffice envelope to each woman. "I went over these yesterday.'' She paused when her phone rang and picked it up. ''Yes?''

''Caryn, I'm sorry, Mr. Preston came in yelling and demanding to see you. He refused to wait for me to ring you,'' Lori said hurriedly. ''He's on his way back there. I already called Security.''

''All right, thanks.'' Caryn took several deep breaths, prepared to tell the others they might want to leave when the door was flung open.

''Hey!'' Pat was on the heels of a large man who strode inside and planted a meaty fist on Caryn's desk.

''You're making trouble where there shouldn't be any, lady,'' he snarled, leaning across the desk toward her. ''You had to write in your fancy magazine that my leotards aren't any good, didn't you? Now all of a sudden my orders are down. Because of you I'm losing business!''

Nothing showed in her demeanor that she was intimidated by the man. ''Mr. Preston, the article had nothing to do with your loss of orders. I'm sure they've been declining for quite some time now and for good reason. Your clothing line is made out of defective material and your guarantee is a joke,'' she stated calmly. She stood up and walked over to a cabinet against one wall, opened it and withdrew a small box. She pulled several pieces of exercise clothing out of the box and tossed them onto the desktop. ''I bought these leotards two months ago. I wore them to my exercise classes, hand washed them with a mild soap and hung them on a line to dry, just as your instructions stated. If you care to look at the seams you will see they are fraying badly and the fabric is faded. I spoke to the manager of a dance-and-exercise shop I patronize. She told me they don't carry your line any longer because there were too many returns and your sales reps gave her a bad time when she brought up the problem. She wanted to return the unsold merchandise and they were downright rude to her. To be blunt, your sales force aren't good representatives of your so-called open policy on returns.''

"You're only talking about one store and two leo-tards. That doesn't say all of them are bad. Maybe you just bought the wrong size." He sneered.

Caryn looked down at her cadet-blue skirt and matching cropped jacket with a blue-and-gold floral print blouse. "Mr. Preston, any problem with your clothing wasn't due to the size, but to the cheap fab-ric you use." She sensed more than saw Sam entering the office and gesturing Tami, Lee and Pat out.

"Is there a problem here, Ms. Richards?" he asked in an equally calm voice.

"Mr. Preston and I were just having a discussion about his merchandise, Mr. Russell, thank you." Her voice was as serene as if she was offering afternoon tea. "And now the man is leaving."

The large man loomed over her. "Lady, this is no discussion. You're ruining me and I'm not going to stand for it."

"Mr. Preston, I think Ms. Richards mentioned that you were on your way out," Sam continued speaking in an even voice, although the light in his eyes was far from calm.

The other man didn't even look at him. "Not until she promises to retract her statement about my cloth-ing."

"We wrote the truth."

He moved threateningly. "You're asking for it."

Mr. Preston may have been a good three inches taller and fifty pounds heavier, but that didn't stop Sam from approaching him and taking his arm in a hold guaranteed to jangle a few nerves.

"I hate to repeat myself, but I do believe the lady asked you to leave." Steel coated his voice. "And as Chief of Security I have a few questions for you, Mr. Preston. If you'll just come with me to my office?"

The man tried to pull away but didn't succeed. "I'm not going anywhere with you!"

"Then we can just call in the police. Besides, all you have to do is answer a few questions to my satisfaction and we won't have any trouble. If you can't, well, that's another story." He ushered the blustering man out with little trouble.

"Whew!" Pat came in looking wide-eyed. "Are you okay?"

Caryn nodded. "He was upset over our review of his clothing line." She dropped the leotards in the wastebasket. "That will save me mailing these to him with my comments."

"Lori said there was no way she could stop him."

She smiled. "Considering the mood he was in, I don't think a Mack truck could have stopped the man."

"Sam did."

"Yes, he certainly did," Caryn acknowledged.

Pat remained in the doorway. "Do you think Mr. Preston has anything to do with the break-ins?"

Caryn shook her head as she walked back to her desk and collapsed in the chair. "I doubt it. The person behind it would be incredibly stupid to confront me to my face. It would be too easy if that were the case. Of course, I wouldn't mind it being solved that smoothly. Then maybe we won't jump every time we open a file drawer or walk into our offices."

"The day I come in and find Pac Man on the computer is the day I hide under the desk and stay there," Pat vowed.

"Believe me, if that happens I'll be joining you under that desk, so leave room for me." Caryn sighed as she looked at the pile of paperwork on her desk. "Where did all of this come from?"

"Most of it you brought in this morning."

She made a face. "You're right. It appears I'll be busy for the rest of the day, so no calls except for important ones, which I'll leave to your discretion."

The secretary nodded as she walked out, closing the door behind her.

Caryn had been hard at work for several hours when Sam strolled into her office and sat down.

"He's clean," he announced without preamble.

She looked up, her reading glasses sliding down to the edge of her nose. "My, my, did you learn that buzz word from 'Dragnet' reruns?"

His expression hardened. "Caryn, the man threatened you because of an article written about his clothing line. I just wanted to make sure he wasn't your vandal. His only crime is manufacturing cheap clothing under an expensive label. Pat said you haven't been out of here since you came in this morning, not even for lunch. Talk about not adhering to a proper diet." He jumped up. "Come on. We're going for a short walk to clear our brains."

She gave him a long-suffering look. "You may have that problem with *your* brain. I don't."

Sam walked over and grabbed her hand, pulling her out of her chair. "You're the one who talks about exercise, so let's indulge in some. I just want you to know I'm doing this for you." He walked out of the office, almost dragging her behind him. "We'll see you in a little while, Pat," he told the surprised secretary.

"Sam, you are a very pushy person," Caryn told him when they rode down in the elevator. "I have more work than I care to think about, and you're dragging me out for a walk you can easily take by yourself."

"Yeah, but it's not as much fun." When they reached the lobby he opened the door for her as they walked outside. "It's just a shame there isn't more fresh air around here."

"Try a drive along the coastline or in the desert," she advised. "You'll find plenty there."

Sam walked along, his hands pushed deep in his slacks pockets. "I called my parents Saturday night to arrange to have my stuff shipped out," he told her. "I bought a bedroom set, a couch, easy chair, coffee table and refrigerator. The refrigerator was the hardest. I didn't realize there were so many on the market. I told the salesman I saw no need to buy one that practically made ice cream by itself when all I needed was something that would keep things cold and give me ice cubes any time I wanted them."

"That must have disappointed him."

"Yeah, he did shed a few tears." Sam abruptly halted and turned to face her, oblivious of people walking around them. "Caryn, are you afraid of me for some reason?"

She gaped at him before she had a chance to reclaim her emotions. "What are you talking about?"

His eyes showed no expression as he smiled blandly. "Nothing. I guess I was just having crazy thoughts."

She looked as if she didn't believe him. "I don't think you've had a crazy thought in your life, even considering the way you act sometimes."

Sam took hold of her arm and turned her in the direction they were originally walking. "Come on, a walk around the block will put roses into your cheeks and whatever else a brisk walk is supposed to do. Besides, after sleeping on an air mattress last night I need this exercise to get the kinks out of my back."

"Why didn't you stay in the hotel until your furniture arrived?"

"Their beds were worse than the air mattress. I got everything else I needed, and the store promised to have my stuff delivered by Wednesday or Thursday, so I can't complain." He grinned.

They finished the rest of their walk in silence. During the ride up in the elevator Caryn was aware of Sam leaning against the wall, his arms crossed in front of his chest, whistling tunelessly as he watched her with a faint smile on his lips. He straightened up when the door opened at her floor.

"Caryn." He placed his hand on her arm to halt her quickly planned escape. "I just want you to know I'm a pretty good listener."

Her head whipped around. "What are you implying?"

He wasn't put off by her stiff manner and frosty tone of voice. "I'm just saying I'm available any time you need a shoulder to lean on, okay? I want to be your friend."

Caryn's chin lifted a fraction of an inch. "I'm sure your offer is well-intentioned, but whatever problems you think I have aren't there. Now I have to return to my work." She moved away from his touch and left him alone in the elevator.

As the elevator zoomed upward to his floor, Sam leaned back against the wall, his hands in his pockets. He didn't like tall women, he reminded himself. He didn't like women who were so independent they saw no need in their lives for a man. So why was he bothering with her so much? What caused him to think about her when he should be concentrating on the job at hand?

"You ignore the obvious, Caryn," he murmured. "So I guess I'll just have to figure out exactly what that problem of yours is. Intruding where I'm not wanted hasn't stopped me before and it certainly won't now."

"I'M SORRY, CARYN, I'm not paid enough to stay here after hours, and if you were smart you wouldn't, either," Pat told her a few minutes after five o'clock.

Caryn smiled. "If that's a hint for a raise you'll have to wait another ten months."

She shrugged. "It never hurts to try. Promise me you won't stay late."

"I promise, Mother," she said with a sigh. "Go on and have a good evening. I just want to approve the next issue before we send it out. It should have been done this afternoon."

Pat's eyes twinkled. "Except you were kidnapped."

"Except I was kidnapped," Caryn repeated.

"He's really a nice guy, Caryn." She turned serious. "Why don't you give him a chance?"

"If you like him that much, he's all yours."

The secretary shook her head. "No thanks, I have an idea he'd be much happier with you. Come on, give the guy a break."

"We're friends, nothing more," Caryn insisted.

"I sure hope I find a friend like that someday. Okay, I get the hint. I'm out the door. Just remember not to stay here too late." She draped the strap of her purse over her shoulder. She turned her head when Tami walked in the door. "'Bye, see you in the morning." She left the two alone.

"This the next issue?" Tami perched her hip on the edge of Caryn's desk. She flicked at the edge of the pages with her fingernail.

"Every hard-worked page of it. It goes into production tomorrow so I want to go over it one final time to make sure everything is in order."

Tami looked disgruntled. "Don't you trust us?"

"Of course I do. It's just an old habit of mine."

Tami straightened. "Yes, but it makes the rest of us feel as if you don't trust us."

Caryn was surprised by her sharp tone. "Tami, it has nothing to do with all of you, so why are you upsetting yourself over something I've been doing since the beginning?"

"Probably because I think I know the reason why you do this. It's because it makes you feel in control," she accused. "You have to feel as if you're in complete charge at all times no matter who you hurt in the meantime. We're not amateurs who have to have every move watched."

Caryn felt glued to her chair. "I'm not that way at all," she said faintly. "Tami, how can you say these things?"

The Eurasian woman shook her head with what looked like disgust and stalked out of the office without saying another word.

Caryn collapsed back in her chair still shaken by the encounter. While the editor had always had a bit of a temper it had never been displayed toward her in such a vehement manner. She buried her face in her hands, trying vainly to ignore the pounding in her head. With a great force of will she sat up straight and returned to her work, but her heart wasn't in it. In the end she merely gave each page a cursory once-over and packaged everything in a large manila envelope.

"Oh, Ms. Richards, I didn't realize you were working late tonight." A lean, spare-featured man stood in the open doorway.

She looked up and smiled at the janitor. "Hi, Larry. Actually, I'm all finished if you need to clean the office." She picked up the envelope and dropped it in her desk drawer, locking it. On her way out she left a note on Pat's desk reminding her she had a breakfast meeting the next day and would be in late and where the proofed work was so it could be sent out first thing.

Not wanting to go home just yet, she stopped by the gym and joined in with an aerobics class that was just beginning and worked out until she felt ready to drop. Only then did she go home and try to relax with a sketch pad and her pastel chalks.

Caryn was feeling the tension begin to leave her body when her doorbell rang. She hesitated, tempted to ignore it when a familiar voice called out.

"Come on, Caryn, I know you're home." Sam's voice rang out loud and clear. "Take pity on me. It's cold out here."

She sighed as she pushed herself away from her drawing board and walked down the stairs.

"And what makes you think I'm in the need of company?" she demanded, standing before him with her hands on her hips.

Sam took in the white jeans and an oversize sweater in a soft aqua shade that skimmed her hips. While the color was flattering to her skin tones he couldn't miss the faint shadows under her eyes and the fatigue in her stance.

"Exercise class again?"

"In order for an exercise regimen to be effective you must perform some kind of aerobic activity three times a week," she loftily intoned.

He rolled his eyes. "That sounds like a magazine article, not you. Besides, you look fine to me." He looked her over from head to toe, but his gaze this time was much warmer and with a masculine appreciation Caryn hadn't seen before.

"Rein in the hormones, Russell," she said sweetly, "or so help me I'll have you evicted before your furniture arrives."

Without bothering to wait for an invitation he brushed by her and entered the living room. He looked up and noticed a light burning in the loft area. He spun around, fixing her with a dark gaze. "You're still working, aren't you? What is it with you, some kind of addiction?"

"The next issue is due to go into production tomorrow. Naturally there's a lot of work involved. What do you think you're doing? Come down from there!"

He ignored her orders and continued up the stairs until he reached the loft. When he saw the drawing board and white layout paper on it he glanced down at her.

"Surprise, surprise," he murmured, moving closer to the board, not hearing Caryn hurry up the stairs and stand behind him. He studied the sketch of a boy running with a dog and looked at the margins where pencil sketches of the boy's face were drawn. "You're very good."

She felt the tightness in her chest expand. "Thank you."

Sam looked at her, an enigmatic expression on his face. "I'd guess very few people know about this."

"It's just a hobby," she murmured.

He was incredulous. "Just a hobby?" He gestured toward her work. "Caryn, you're very talented. I admit I'm no art expert, but I like what I see here. Don't downgrade yourself by saying it isn't very good or just something you do in your spare time."

"I told you before it's only a hobby," she said, enunciating her words slowly. "I draw pictures for friends and for my own pleasure, nothing else." Her eyes met his squarely and it was clear she wasn't going to back off.

His brow creased. "Who is the real Caryn Richards? The woman in the office with her power trip and no-nonsense attitude, or the woman in the home with soft colors surrounding her? Maybe you should do some heavy thinking and decide which one you want to be."

"I'm very tired. Thank you for stopping by."

Sam wasn't fazed by her cool words. He smiled mockingly and walked down the stairs not looking back once. In a moment the front door closed behind him.

Caryn dropped onto her chair, feeling the tremors wash over her body.

"He's making me lose control and I can't allow it," she said between clenched teeth. "I *won't* allow it." Just as quickly she stood up and walked down the stairs. "I won't lose control," she kept repeating to herself as she entered the kitchen. "I won't."

"HOW WAS YOUR BREAKFAST?" Pat asked when Caryn walked in.

She looked at her warily. "Is this a trick question or do you have bad news for me?"

"You left me a note saying that the pages were in your bottom drawer."

Caryn fought the dread feelings welling up inside. "That's right. I put them there right before I left."

Pat shook her head. "Caryn, they're not there."

She fought the urge to scream. "Are you sure you looked in the bottom drawer?" She walked swiftly into her office and opened the drawer, rummaging through the contents. She continued searching each drawer with no success. "Have you talked to anyone else?"

"I wanted to ask you first. Did Tami see you put it there?"

"I put it here!" Caryn snapped, then apologized. "Sorry, it's just so frustrating. No, she didn't. She had gone on her high horse and picked a fight. She left before I did."

The two women's eyes met with a silent question floating between them.

"Tami may have a temper, but she isn't vindictive," Pat insisted.

Caryn hoped so. "Was she here before you?"

Pat nodded, looking miserable at having to bring it up. "She left a note on my desk saying that she lost a telephone number but couldn't find my Rolodex. Since our problems began I've been locking it away at night. Caryn, she may have been angry with you, but she would never do something like this."

Caryn sighed, pressing her fingertips against her forehead. "I'm going to talk to the others. Maybe they can come up with something. Damn! I know I put it in there and it has to go out today!"

"Our little demon," Pat muttered. "How much do you want to bet that's who's behind this?"

She swore more forcefully. "I don't need it today." Shrugging off her coat, she hung it up and put away her purse before leaving her office. Within a short period of time she had spoken to everyone, leaving Tami for last.

"You think I did it, don't you?" She looked at her boss suspiciously. "You think I hid the envelope out of pure spite."

"Tami, you may be a lot of things, but you're not spiteful," Caryn argued. "All I'm asking is if you saw anything or anyone unusual either last night or this morning."

"Nothing." Her eyes softened. "Look, Caryn, I know we have our differences on magazine policy and we'll probably keep on fighting, but sabotage isn't my style."

"Pat seems to think it's our little friend again." She rubbed her forehead wishing she had taken some aspirin before embarking on the search. "Then how did he or she get into my desk? Pat or I would have seen scratch marks on the surface if the lock had been forced. How could someone get a key to my desk?"

"If they can get in and out of here without being noticed, they can do anything. What do we do now?"

Caryn had already come up with a possible solution. "Everyone goes through their files with a fine-tooth comb. I'm hoping this time it's just mischief, and the person decided to deliberately leave it in someone else's file to throw us off instead of destroying it. That way we would naturally make new copies of everything, which would put us behind schedule. Eventually the envelope would show up making us even angrier with ourselves and one another."

Tami nodded. "I sure hope this creep thought that way, because we couldn't put everything back together again in short order. You want me to spread the word?"

Caryn shook her head. "I already asked the others. They aren't happy about it and I can't blame them, but I prefer trying that tactic first. I'm even going through all my files."

An hour later Pat entered Caryn's office with a strange look on her face and holding the infamous envelope.

"So our little office demon did what I thought he or she would do," Caryn said looking relieved. "Where was it found?"

Pat didn't smile. "In Tami's inactive files."

Chapter Six

"Caryn, this is a frame—some kind of sick joke—and I'm the victim!" Tami shouted, pacing from one end of the office to the other. "Someone else took the envelope and hid it in my files to make me look bad." Her long dark hair swished around her waist every time she made a turn.

"Why would someone want to do that?" Sam sounded as matter-of-fact as if he had just asked her about the weather.

"How should I know? To make even more trouble, to make me look bad in everyone's eyes. I don't know!" Her face was red and blotchy with fury.

Caryn sat on the couch looking as sick as she felt. She hadn't expected Sam to walk in just as she had begun asking Tami how she'd happened to find the envelope, which had been quickly checked over and sent out. He said Lori told him what happened and he preferred sitting in. Tami took it as their assuming her guilty until she could prove her innocence. As a result she reacted in her usual hellfire manner.

"Tami, I never thought you took it," Caryn broke in. "One thing you've always been with me is upfront. If you have a problem you've always come to me so we can talk it out or yell it out, whatever the case may be. This kind of malicious prank isn't your style."

She spun around, staring at her boss with hope in her dark eyes. "Then you believe me?"

"Yes, I do. I have to admit the evidence against you is damning, but I don't think you did it. I almost feel as if this person is trying to turn us against one another. And if we're not careful he or she will succeed."

Tami's fury evaporated as quickly as it had appeared.

"Why do you think someone chose you to be the scapegoat?" Sam questioned.

"Because it's well-known that Tami and I have our differences of opinion. Therefore, what better person to pin something on? I would naturally blame her and we'd probably have a blowup ending with either my firing her or her quitting," Caryn explained.

Tami winced at the idea, murmuring, "I don't even want to think about that happening."

He turned to Caryn. "How well-known are your battles? Would any outsider know of this?"

The two women's eyes locked. Tami was the one to answer. "No. It's almost an inside joke that Caryn and I agree to disagree on a regular basis. We decided long ago that it keeps the air clear between us."

"So why would you feel this was deliberate?" he asked.

Tami shrugged. "Probably because that was the first thing I thought of, especially since..." Her voice dropped as she realized what she was going to say next. Her eyes, full of panic, met Caryn's silently, questioning whether to finish the sentence truthfully or end it differently.

"Especially since Tami and I had an argument last night," Caryn said, finishing the sentence for her.

"How many people know about this argument you two had?" Sam asked.

The two women looked at each other and shook their heads.

"Everyone else had already left," Caryn replied.

He looked at one then the other. "Then give me a good reason why someone would pin this sick joke on Tami?"

"Perhaps she was chosen at random, and it just happened to cause more trouble than the person expected it would," Caryn told him, trying to think of anything that would make the least bit of sense. Ever since she had come into work that morning she felt as if she were riding a roller coaster. Would this never end? she cried out inside. "Sam, we found the envelope and got it off, so hopefully we haven't lost too much time. To be honest that's all that counts to me, and that's all that will matter to Mr. Gregory."

There was nothing of the charming rogue about him now as he stared at her long and hard before speaking in cold tones. "Caryn, this person is getting more serious every time. If you hadn't found that envelope quickly you would have lost time and money. And you know how Mr. Gregory is about money. He wants to make it, not lose it because he feels someone isn't doing their job properly."

"Believe me, I know Mr. Gregory's philosophies quite well," she said tightly, her eyes flashing with quick anger. "Mr. Gregory will receive a full report regarding this matter."

"That's all right, this one *I'll* file." Sam stood up, his rising temper evident in his stiff figure.

"The problem was solved internally. Therefore I'll take care of it," Caryn stood up, pleased she could look him in the eye, thanks to her high heels, and equally pleased he appeared to not like the idea.

Sam's jaw clenched. "Don't step on my toes, Caryn. Believe me, I can get nasty when someone treads where they shouldn't. You wouldn't like that side of me at all."

"If you don't want your toes stepped on, stay in your office where you don't have to worry about it happening."

He shot her one more fulminating look before stalking out of her office.

"Talk about sparks flying," Tami muttered, pleased she had been witness to their argument. "And people think you and I fight."

"I have an idea this upset is nothing compared to what he could do if he really lost his temper," Caryn said wearily. "First thing on the agenda is to have someone come in today and change the locks on everyone's file drawers. The scary part is that there weren't any scratch marks on my drawer or yours, meaning this person is either an expert at picking locks or somehow got copies of the keys. From now on, any important work in progress will be put in the office safe. Nothing will be kept out in the open. If necessary, we'll even change computer codes daily."

"Do you think that will give us any protection? For all we know they might have the combination to the safe and he might be an expert when it comes to computers," Tami said.

Caryn sighed, wishing for a much easier solution, although she knew one wasn't available at the moment. "It's either that or carry the work home with us every night. As it is the next prank will probably be of a different nature. It seems to work out that way."

Tami nodded. She started to leave the office then turned back, offering her boss a tentative smile. "Caryn, thank you for believing in me."

She smiled. "We all have to stick together in this, Tami. This is a battle none of us can afford to lose."

The editor smiled back and left the office. Pat entered immediately, carrying a coffee mug and thrust it at Caryn.

"Drink it," she ordered.

Caryn took a healthy swallow and began coughing as the liquid hit her stomach with an unexpected jolt.

"What is in this?" she gasped, wide-eyed.

"Brandy."

"Brandy?" she choked, putting the cup down. "Why on earth did you put brandy in the coffee?"

"Medicinal purposes. You looked white as a sheet," she said crisply. "Now you have some color in your cheeks."

Caryn put her palms against her face, feeling alcohol-induced warmth against her hands. "I'm sure I do."

"What now, boss lady?" Pat picked up the mug and handed it back to her. "Drink all of it."

"That's it, get me drunk so I can't accomplish anything for the rest of the day," she muttered, taking a more cautious sip this time, feeling a delicious warmth roll down her throat. "Would you please do me a favor and set up times for me to meet with everyone on a private basis? I want to take a minimum of a half hour with each person."

Pat nodded. "Do you want the meetings to start today? Or are you willing to begin tomorrow when you feel more like yourself?"

"Today. I hate to think how many people heard about Tami and learned Sam was asking her questions." Her voice hardened. "I'm not going to let some crazy try to cast any blame on my people again."

Caryn's first meeting turned out to be with Jodi, and deciding to talk away from the office, they left the building for lunch. While she was gone Sam appeared. A suspicious Lori allowed him to go back to speak with Pat after frostily informing him Caryn had left the office.

"You've got guts coming back here so soon," Pat greeted him as he walked up to her desk and leaned over, planting his hands on the top.

"I was doing my job," he retorted.

"So was Caryn and she knows these people much better than you do. Right now she's at a luncheon meeting. Do us all a favor and don't be here when she gets back. She needs to recover from all this."

He nodded. "Lori already told me she wasn't here. Besides, I figured you could help me with a couple of questions I have."

She looked at him suspiciously. "Such as?"

"Who has keys to the desks and file cabinets?"

Pat thought for a moment. "Each of us has keys to our own desks, and I have a master set that is kept in my desk."

"And your desk is locked whenever you're away from it?"

She laughed. "Of course not. That would be too much of a hassle. It's only locked at night." Then it dawned on her. "You think someone got to the master set when I wasn't here?"

"It would be very easy for someone to have a look around when you're gone for lunch or if you happen to be away from your desk for a length of time. After all, you wouldn't have a reason to check for the keys during the day, would you?"

Pat inhaled. "No, I wouldn't. Oh boy. It's getting scary, Sam."

He nodded. "I have a couple of people helping me go over that list you gave me. I'm hoping we'll come up with something from that. One thing I should have asked you earlier. Did anyone ever threaten Caryn or the magazine? I'm not talking about the usual empty threats someone in the heat of anger might issue, but a real bonafide threat that could really scare a person. I'd ask Caryn, but I don't think she wants to talk to me right now."

"You're right, she wouldn't," Pat said bluntly. "Off the top of my head I can't think of anyone. Sure there've been a few who've made threats in the past. The owner of one spa with inexperienced staff told Caryn she'd be sorry for the article we'd written—he'd had to close down the spa not long after the issue came out—but that's usually what we hear. Just as you said that kind of threat is harmless, just someone letting off steam."

His interest sharpened. "What kind of article?"

"The kind comparing health spas," she explained. "We run ads for health spas in the back of the magazine. We had several women write in with complaints about Sunset Ridge spa, stating it was more beauty treatments than helping a person lose weight. One woman told us the instructors didn't seem to know what they were doing and couldn't answer the simplest questions dealing with fitness. Caryn was suspicious and since the spa was near Palm Springs, not all that far from L.A., she decided to send someone in. One of our free-lance writers volunteered, saying she'd like to visit several spas and see what kind of programs were offered. Sunset Ridge spa was a joke—the diet wasn't as low-calorie as it should be for someone trying to lose weight, and every beauty treatment was an additional fee. She was able to gain the confidence of one of the instructors and found out the woman wasn't qualified, just someone who learned aerobics from watching exercise tapes. Our free-lance writer wrote up an article comparing five spas, and naturally Sunset Ridge came out at rock bottom.''

Sam nodded. ''Let me have all the names. I'd like to check them out further.''

Pat nodded as she turned to her computer terminal. ''We're lucky there. It should only take a few minutes for me to bring up the information.''

Sam later pocketed the sheet of paper and thanked Pat. ''I owe you a lunch for this,'' he told her.

''You also owe Caryn an apology for upsetting her this morning,'' Pat called after him.

He waved over his shoulder. ''She's a big girl, Pat. And this is business.''

When Caryn later returned to her office she found a large bouquet of flowers set in the middle of her credenza.

''They arrived a few minutes ago,'' Pat told her.

She looked puzzled and just a bit wary, which was understandable considering the events of the past few weeks. ''Who are they from?''

"I wouldn't dream of reading a card addressed to you," she said airily. "You'll have to find out the identity yourself."

"I hope you called the bomb squad," Caryn said dryly, plucking the square white card from the arrangement and sliding her nail under the flap.

I'm not one for apologies, so I'm sending these in hopes of softening your mood. Hopefully you won't bring out the shotgun next time I come calling.

Sam

"Wow," Pat breathed, looking over her shoulder. She held her hands up in surrender when Caryn scowled at her. "Just because I didn't read it before didn't mean I wouldn't try now. I told you the man liked you."

Caryn kept staring at the flowers. "No one's ever sent me flowers before," she whispered, touching one colorful blossom with reverent fingertips. "Corsages for dances, but I've never received anything like this. Why would he do this after all our fighting earlier?"

"Maybe he thought he came down too hard on you," Pat pointed out. "Tell me something. Has he asked you out yet?"

"No. And I don't think he will, not that it matters to me." She hadn't told anyone about helping him find a place to live and she wasn't about to. Pat had it in her head to find Caryn a man, even as she complained there weren't any good ones around for her, and if she knew about that Saturday she'd start asking Sam if his intentions were honorable.

"You already told him you were off limits, didn't you?" she guessed. At the expression on Caryn's face she threw her hands up in disgust. "Caryn, you're hopeless."

"If you think he's that great why don't you go after him for yourself?" Caryn found herself tired of this conversation. She leafed through her phone messages. "Isn't that new model coming in this afternoon?"

Pat sighed, recognizing the reason for the switch in conversation. "She'll be here at two-thirty."

Caryn started to walk into her office then halted on the threshold. "Pat, I consider you my friend as well as my secretary, but I don't need or want a man in my life. Please stop playing Cupid."

"Before you pull rank? Okay. After all, who knows? Sam might be the type to eat crackers in bed, or worse."

"I'm sure it would be much worse. Buzz me when the model arrives." She walked into her office and immediately headed for the tiny bathroom set off to one side. She desperately needed to splash some cold water on her face.

SAM WAS SITTING behind his desk, his feet propped on top as he leaned far back in his chair.

"Some authoritative figure you are." Brian, one of his top investigators, entered the office. Sam had felt pleased when Brian chose to leave the Chicago office and move west with him.

"If you had knocked first I would have taken my feet off my desk and looked extremely authoritative." He grinned, unabashed. "Whatcha got for me?"

The other man tossed a sheet of paper on Sam's desk. "Jerome Jenkins owned the Sunset Ridge health spa near Palm Springs. He hired kids off the street, promising them good money and instant qualifications as fitness experts, along with telling them they could later apply for jobs in his spas in Europe."

"Which he doesn't have."

"Which he doesn't have," Brian echoed. "One woman's skin was burned from some kind of revolutionary European body masque. That's only one of many lawsuits against the guy. *Simple Fitness*'s article was just another problem for him. I'll be honest with you, Sam, I don't think he's the one behind the magazine's vandalism. Jenkins is strictly small-time. Not to mention he skipped the country a month after he closed the spa down. He was last heard of trying to start another bogus one in the Bahamas. I gather he puts up a pretty image for the ladies and they lap up every phony word."

Sam closed his eyes. "I should have known that would have been too easy for us. What else have you got?"

"So far, zip. We both know people make idle threats when they're angry. And that's what most of these have turned out to be. Chad's almost finished with his list of spas and we're going into another category. Oh, I also finished a more thorough check on Mr. Personality Preston. His only crime is using cheap fabric for his clothing line and acting like a complete jerk. I also made a quick sweep of the offices of the editors during the lunch hour. No one locks their doors, desks or files. Of course, they probably don't see the need to. Normally I would agree. The side entrance is also kept unlocked, and anyone could slip through there without being seen if they happened to time it right. I'll tell you, Sam, this is pretty bad."

He sighed as he reached up and loosened his tie. "Well, whether they like it or not they're going to have to tighten their security measures down there or the old man will be on them like glue. None of this makes sense, Brian."

Brian nodded as he stood up. "Just out of personal interest—do you have plans for Caryn Richards?"

Sam's head snapped up so fast it cracked. "Caryn? Why?"

Brian smiled at his suspicious tone. "She's a nice-looking lady and I thought about asking her out to dinner."

"She doesn't eat dinner. She exercises," he muttered.

Unperturbed, Brian went on, "So I'll ask her if she wouldn't mind having company while she works out and we can go to dinner afterward." He looked at Sam's closed features. "You don't mind, do you?"

"Why should I mind? She's a free agent," Sam mumbled, showing undue interest in a report. "It has nothing to do with me."

Brian smiled. "Yeah."

Sam didn't look up until he knew he was alone. "If I don't mind why do I feel as if I do?" he asked himself. "She's a pretty lady, a bit bullheaded for my taste and definitely too tall. So why don't I want Brian taking her out?"

"If you don't quit talking to yourself I'm calling the men in the white coats," his secretary called out.

"Give me a second and I'll even look up their number for you," Sam said.

SAM WAS SURPRISED when he saw Caryn's lights come on while he stood at the kitchen sink eating a messy burrito he had picked up on the way home from the office. Without thinking twice, he quickly finished and hurried across the walkway.

"Hi," he greeted her with a disarming grin when she opened the door to his knock.

"Hi, yourself. By rights I should slam this in your face," she informed him, leaning against the doorjamb. "Would you like to give me a good reason why I shouldn't?"

"I could be crass and tell you how much I spent on your flowers."

Caryn gave him a look that told him she knew exactly what kind of man he was. "Tell me something about yourself I don't already know."

"I thought you might have gone out by now." Sam mentally kicked himself for saying it.

She looked at him quizzically. "Why would you think that?"

"Maybe because Brian Palmer mentioned he was going to ask you out for a night of dinner and debauchery," he said with an air of nonchalance.

A faint smile lifted the corners of her mouth. "He did ask me out, although he didn't mention anything about the latter."

"Oh." Sam tried to look cheerful. "So you're going out with him this weekend."

"Sam, my private life isn't any of your business," Caryn said firmly. "Unless you feel there's a good reason why I shouldn't go out with Brian?"

He flushed. "Oh, no, he's a great guy. He jogs every morning, works out three or four times a week and wouldn't allow red meat to pass his lips. Just your type.''

"Would it make you feel better if I said that I told Brian I don't feel I should see anyone on a social basis while we're having so much trouble at the magazine? Because that's exactly what I did tell him. And he was very understanding about it and not pushy, like some other people I know.''

"I'm not pushy," he defended himself. "Just concerned for your well-being.''

"Of course you are." Her sardonic tone indicated she knew it was something entirely different. "Look, Sam, it's very nice of you to come by and check on me, although there was no reason for you to, because I've done very well on my own for the past ten years. Good night, Sam.''

He winced, remembering her earlier warning that she didn't want to get too chummy with her neighbors, especially ones she worked with.

"Sorry about that, I guess I forgot the rules," he said quietly. "Good night, Caryn.''

WHEN SAM ENTERED the building lobby he noticed Caryn and Jodi talking, before Jodi headed for the elevator and Caryn left the building.

"Hi there," Jodi greeted him with a broad smile. "You just missed the boss lady.''

"I think she'll survive.''

Jodi bit down on her lower lip to keep from smiling. "Rumor has it you're renting the town house across from Caryn.''

"Rumors are always correct." He stood back to allow her to enter the car first.

Jodi shot him a sideways look. "Don't tell me she won't go out with you."

"I haven't asked," Sam replied.

"Brian Palmer did and she shot him down very effectively."

His interest pricked up. "Really?"

"My, don't we look unhappy about it," Jodi teased. "There are many facets to Caryn's personality, and most people don't care to delve any deeper than the surface."

He looked at her. "You sound more like a psychologist than a fashion editor."

"I took several psychology classes," she admitted. "Sometimes helping a person eat properly takes more than drawing up a diet. I also need to find a good motivation for them. So, I tend to look deeper into a person. Such as, did you notice what Caryn was wearing today?"

Sam shrugged. "A suit in some kind of brown color."

Jodi rolled her eyes. "Some kind of brown? What kind of investigator are you? Her suit is a very strong shade of cinnamon. And as her neighbor I wouldn't be surprised if you've seen the inside of her house."

He nodded, seeing the direction of her thoughts. When the elevator stopped at her floor they both got off and stood near the door. "Her town house is done in soft colors. And she wears pastel colors when she's home."

Jodi smiled. "Exactly. At work, Caryn wears strong colors that give her a no-nonsense image. It's as if she has two different personalities and she refuses to allow the two to blend in a pleasing harmony. I took several courses in colors relating to a person's personality and life-style. Ironically, Caryn doesn't fit any set image. Don't you find that interesting?" She smiled broadly.

Sam looked puzzled. "What does all this have to do with me?"

Jodi continued smiling. "One very interesting fact. Caryn didn't mind that you became a neighbor and you've seen the inside of her house. Her last relationship was more than two years ago, and while she never said very much about it we could tell the breakup wasn't mutual and it hit her very hard." Her smile disappeared. "We all like Caryn and we don't want to see her hurt. I'm just hoping you'll be the one to bring her back to the true land of the living. Okay?"

Sam held up his hands, palms out. "Hey, count me out. The lady has her own idea on how to live her life, and she would prefer I keep to myself. I'm beginning to think I'd be better off if I did."

Jodi tipped her head to one side, looking him over from head to toe. "Have you ever done what you're expected to do?"

He looked all too innocent. "No."

"Then do yourself a favor, because I'm certain you won't regret it. Go ahead and sweep Caryn off her feet. I don't think you'd regret it."

"She's not my type," he argued.

Jodi shook her head. "Give me some credit, Sam Russell. I've seen the way you look at her. Just pour on the charm. You two will make a lovely couple. Think Cary Grant. You'll do fine." She patted him on the shoulder and walked into the magazine's offices.

"I look lousy in a tuxedo," he called after her.

Chapter Seven

"First of all, I'd like to make it clear that I'm not suggesting we go out on a date this weekend," were the first words out of Sam's mouth when Caryn answered the phone.

She was puzzled by his abrupt statement. "Then why are you calling me?"

"I need to pick up some stuff for my place, and a few people in the office suggested I try the flea market at the Rose Bowl and look around at yard sales," he replied. "I was hoping you'd take pity on me and go along to help me pick out something suitable."

Caryn sighed. He would discover her weakness. She enjoyed nothing more than finding a good yard sale or going to the swap meet and seeing what obscure item she could discover.

"We'll need to get an early start," he warned. "I'll pick you up at eight on Saturday morning." He hung up before she had a chance to say no.

Sam grinned to himself as he replaced the receiver in the cradle. "Cary Grant couldn't have done any better, and I don't have to worry about wearing a tux, either," he murmured, sounding very pleased with himself.

Promptly at eight o'clock Sam stood on Caryn's doorstep. She walked out, hooking a large canvas bag over her shoulder.

"Is that for your makeup?" he said with a deadpan face, staring at the bag.

She playfully punched his shoulder. "Very funny. Believe me, this comes in really handy at the swap meet. You'll see."

Sam looked from her swinging ponytail down to her worn running shoes. "Something tells me that you're an expert at this."

"Ask anyone at the magazine and they'll moan and groan about the times I coaxed one of them to go along with me." Caryn dropped her keys into a zippered pocket inside her bag. "You'd be amazed at the excuses I hear when I mention going to yard sales or the swap meet and ask if anyone wants to go along."

"And here I thought you lived and breathed the magazine, even on the weekend," he murmured, keeping in step with her back to his garage. "Lady, you're full of surprises."

She shook her head. "For me it's a nice way to relax. Tami once wrote an article about mall walking, which is becoming a popular way of getting exercise for those who can't indulge in anything too energetic. She asked me to write a sidebar about my experiences walking through a swap meet and hitting the block sales. I had suggested that if they didn't want to go broke they leave their money at home." She slid into the passenger seat of Sam's Mustang. "We got some very favorable response on it."

He frowned. "Do you look at everything you do as some kind of exercise?"

She was surprised by his question. "Not really. I guess it just works out that way."

"Eight to five, Monday through Friday, yes. But the evenings and weekends should be yours, not the magazine's." Sam shifted gears with a bit more force than needed. "Today, we're doing this for fun, not for exercise. Understood?"

Caryn turned her head, seeing the granite lines of his jaw and sharp-bladed nose. "All right." She couldn't understand why he was taking such a forceful point of view, but she wasn't in the mood to argue.

Following Caryn's directions, Sam parked in the huge parking area for the Rose Bowl, more known for its New Year's Day college football game than the other events that took place during the rest of the year.

"I think it would be fun to attend a Rose Bowl game one year," Sam commented, as they walked toward one of the entrances. He looked around at the crowds, noticing most of the people were carrying large shopping bags. He lowered his head to say in her ear. "This is incredible. That bag of yours is nothing compared to what some of these people bring along to carry their stuff home in."

Caryn reached inside her tote and pulled out a folded paper shopping bag, with a handle, found in department stores. "Oh, I'm prepared."

After they entered the grounds, they stood off to one side before deciding where to start.

"What exactly are you looking for?" Caryn asked him.

Sam shrugged. "Oh, some pictures, maybe some fake plants."

"Why not real ones?"

"I've never been home long enough to try keeping a real plant alive," he said. "Let's look at the fake ones first. A couple of lamps wouldn't hurt, either. I don't know, whatever grabs my interest, I guess. Where shall we start?" He looked around, unable to grasp the acres of bargains before him.

"Our best bet is to start at the first row and work our way through."

Sam took Caryn's hand so they couldn't be separated by the crowding and pushing people as they battled their way over to the first row. At least, that was the reason he gave her. Deep inside, he knew it was just a good excuse to touch her.

"If you see something you like we'll keep track in here." She held out a small notebook she'd dug out of her bag. "Admittedly, if you feel it's something you can't live without you're better off buying it right away. A few times I found something and decided to wait and came back only to find it sold."

Sam grabbed hold of one end of her bag and pulled it toward him. "What do you have in there?" He pretended to bury his head inside. "I can't believe this! Were you planning on going away for a few days?" He pulled out a soft blue pullover sweater, hairbrush and makeup bag before diving back for more.

"Leave that alone!" She hit his rummaging hand hard enough to cause him to yelp. "I swear you're worse than a small child."

"I'll probably have a bruise," he grumbled, nursing his sore hand as they began walking up the first row.

Everywhere Sam looked he found something that he couldn't resist buying. "If I make the loft into a den this would go there perfectly," he announced, holding up his latest find.

Caryn winced as she studied a tall table lamp that, as far as she was concerned, had no redeeming qualities. While the shade appeared old-fashioned with its dark green fabric covering and heavy fringe, the base was the hourglass shape of a nude woman.

"I have never seen anything this ugly," she decided out loud. "Having something like that in your home will guarantee people coming to visit you once and never returning." She lowered her voice so the vendor wouldn't hear her. "Sam, that lamp is so ugly it isn't even funny. Even a junk dealer wouldn't want it."

"Ugly?" He examined the lamp more closely. "Are you kidding? When I was a kid I used to dream about women shaped like this. This lamp is a reminder of one of my favorite daydreams."

"Women with figures like that went out with whalebone corsets." Caryn grabbed his hand and dragged him away from the booth before he gave in. "Come on, I'm sure we can find something you'll like just as well, if not more."

He gave the lamp one last lingering look. "Caryn, you didn't even give it a chance. It would grow on you."

"Moss grows on you, too, but that doesn't mean I'll give it a chance." She halted to examine a booth filled with hand-knitted sweaters. "My vice. I have more sweaters at home than I'll probably ever wear." She studied an intarsia design of bronze, cream and honey. "This is perfect." In no time the sweater was folded neatly in the bottom of her shopping bag along with a brighter-colored one she intended to be a birthday gift for her mother.

It was more than an hour later that Sam found a lamp that also met Caryn's approval. He paid for it and asked if he could pick it up on his way out. They continued walking down each row, occasionally stopping to examine an everyday item they couldn't live without or something so bizarre they enjoyed figuring out its use.

"I have to have one," he announced, pulling her toward a booth a short distance away.

Caryn looked bewildered, not seeing his destination right away. "Have what? Oh, Sam, no. This is definitely something you don't need. Believe me, I would put up with that awful lamp before one of these."

He gazed over the display of carved wooden guns that shot rubber bands instead of bullets with the avidness of a small boy. "I can set up a target in the office," he mused, examining each gun with great care before picking up one that shot two rubber bands. "Look at this, will you?"

Caryn stared at the toy as if the last thing she wanted to do was touch it. "Do you realize how dangerous that could be?"

Sam shook his head. "I don't intend to shoot people with it, only a target on the wall when I get frustrated." He hefted the carved weapon in his hand before putting it down an picking up another.

The vendor, sensing he had a serious customer, approached them and extolled the virtue of each gun.

"This is great," Sam said excitedly, finally selecting a gun that shot one band at a time.

"How old did you say you were?" Caryn asked dryly after they left the booth with Sam's newest purchase in her shopping bag.

He comically leered at her. "Old enough to ogle the girls. Come on, let's get something to eat."

"You can if you want. I just want something cold to drink," she replied. "All this walking has made me thirsty."

"You need more than that," he remonstrated. "We've been here for hours and it's way past the lunch hour."

Caryn laughed. "Sam, some people's stomachs don't go by a time clock the way yours does."

He shook his head, amused and frustrated by her attitude. Taking her hand he pulled her toward an eating area, and without consulting her ordered hot dogs, French fries and sodas for each of them.

"Don't worry, it's diet soda," he told her, handing her the drinks before they looked for a place to sit.

Seated on the molded plastic seat, Caryn cocked her head to one side, studying the man sitting across from her. "I never would have guessed you were a tyrant at heart."

"Everyone has their secrets." He took a big bite out of his hot dog.

"And what's yours?"

Sam chewed, reflecting on her question. After swallowing he leaned forward as if imparting a great secret. "I've lusted after Kathleen Turner since I saw her in *Body Heat*."

Caryn nodded. "Now I know you're crazy."

He shook his head. "Nope, I'm just a guy who knows when to relax. My work is frustrating at times, involves a great deal of concentration, and there's no time for mistakes, but we still make them. I'm not a party animal, and my idea of hard drugs is Extra

Strength Tylenol. So if I go off the wall occasionally I figure I'm better off than a lot of people.''

Caryn leaned back, seeing much more in his words than perhaps he intended. ''You enjoy having people think you're more than a bit abnormal, because that way you can catch them off guard.''

He shrugged. ''To be honest, I don't care how people see me. It has nothing to do with catching someone off guard. As far as I'm concerned, it's how I perceive myself that counts.'' He suddenly laughed. ''Hey, how did we get off on such a serious subject? Come on, tell me one of your secrets,'' he coaxed. ''After all, I told you one of mine.''

''You told me your secret lust,'' she corrected. ''Big difference.''

''Okay, tell me your secret lust. I'm not choosy.''

If Sam hadn't been the observant man he was, he wouldn't have noticed the way her expression closed for just a fraction of a second. Just as suddenly, her expression cleared and she leaned across the table in the exact same way he had, her eyelids coyly lowered.

''He may not be considered a hotshot star and sex symbol, but I wouldn't object if Pee-wee Herman carried me off for a wild and decadent weekend.'' Her husky whisper was enough to send shivers up and down a man's spine, especially Sam's as he visualized the kind of getaway she mentioned.

Sam looked at her warily. ''I admit that isn't who I would have chosen for you.'' He sincerely hoped she was joking but was afraid she wasn't.

''To each his own.'' She favored him with a slow and sexy smile and saucy wink.

Without even thinking about what she was doing, Caryn hastily finished her lunch and stood up. "We have a lot of walking ahead of us."

Sam stood, gathering up Caryn's bag, ignoring her protests. "It's only fair I carry it some of the time, since a good part of the purchases are mine," he explained, transferring the bag to his other hand. "Let's see how much more damage I can do to my wallet."

In the end, Sam appeared to restrain himself as he found a throw rug for the kitchen floor in front of the sink and several silk plants for the living room. He stopped by one of the first booths they had visited and expressed disappointment that the lamp with the nude for a base was gone.

"That just goes to show you that someone has good taste," he informed her as they walked out to the parking lot, crowded with people heading for their cars. "I missed out on the buy of a lifetime."

Caryn rolled her eyes. "Maybe so, but if you had wanted it so badly you would have bought it no matter what I said."

Sam halted in front of his car and placed one hand on the hood. "You said if I bought it no one would come to visit me twice. I didn't want you to have that excuse."

She halted and stared at him. She saw no teasing, no hint of amusement in his eyes or on his face. She licked suddenly dry lips.

"You're trying to complicate things, Sam."

"Complicate what? What do you see between us other than the beginnings of a friendship?" he pressed.

"You know very well what I mean." Caryn's voice sounded high pitched.

"Do I? Then maybe I'm missing something here." His stance was watchful. "Why don't you fill me in?"

Without saying another word, Caryn walked around to the passenger side and waited for him to unlock the door. After a moment Sam did so. He walked around to the rear of the car and tossed the bags into the trunk, laying the lamp carefully on top, using a blanket he had back there to cushion it against the bumps. When he slid behind the steering wheel he didn't start the engine immediately, but sat there with his arms draped over the wheel.

"Caryn, I'm not trying to pick a fight with you," he said quietly. "I enjoyed today a great deal and I hope we can do this again. It's just that I feel you back off the minute you think I'm crowding you. Look, all I want to do is have days like this, maybe sometime go out to dinner or a movie." He turned his head, "Okay?"

"Didn't we have a similar conversation not long ago?" She preferred not looking directly at those pale blue eyes that saw too much.

He frowned. "I want to be your friend, Caryn. Why is that so hard for you to accept?"

She lifted the end of her ponytail off her back. "Men friends have trouble sticking to their bargain. They always want more."

"Don't categorize me, Caryn." With that Sam switched on the engine and backed out of the space with skill, evading the cars racing down the aisle in their quest for the exit.

After leaving the Rose Bowl, Sam found himself loath to get on the freeway and head for home.

"Are you in a hurry to get home?" he asked, nothing in his tone to indicate his mood.

She looked at him, surprised by his change of mood. "Not really, why?"

"How would you feel about driving through the older part of Pasadena and gawking at the big houses?"

"A lot of times all you'll see are closed gates and security signs," she warned. "The houses are usually so far back from the gate you only see trees."

"Fine. I can see what security companies they use."

"Why?"

Sam shrugged as he halted at the red traffic light and signaled a left turn. "Sometimes I think about going out on my own, especially days when old man Gregory is threatening to disembowel me for not doing things fast enough. Then there're days I realize how nice it is to have a paycheck coming in on a regular basis and not having to worry if I can make the rent. So it's easier to put up with his tantrums and threats and get the job done my way."

Caryn thought of the unknown perpetrator in her office and shuddered. "Without clues there's no chance of catching the person, is there?" she whispered, not even seeing the beautiful three-story adobe home on her right.

"There're clues—I just have to figure them out. The same way you figure out an intricate puzzle," he replied. "Don't worry, he or she will trip up sooner or later, and I'll be there."

"And if the pranks suddenly stop?"

Sam didn't want to tell Caryn he didn't think they would until someone ended up seriously hurt, perhaps even Caryn herself. He still felt that Caryn might have the answer and just didn't know it. He only wished he knew how to find it.

"Then we'll have one less thing to worry about, won't we? Look at that house. How much money do you think it would take to make a decent down payment?" He pointed out a colonial-style house that could have doubled as a small mansion.

Caryn turned her head to study the house. "I don't think we'd live that long."

"That's what I thought."

Sam drove around for another hour before asking if Caryn was ready for dinner.

"Dinner? We just had lunch."

He flashed her a telling look. "Lunch was around five hours ago, and I walked mine off in no time. Come on, that place looks good." He pulled into a nearby restaurant.

Caryn would have settled for a salad, but Sam wasn't having it. After announcing he was more than willing to pay the tab after all the help she'd given him that day and she could have anything she desired, he practically bullied her into having a steak along with her salad. After they ate, Caryn pleaded fatigue and was relieved Sam didn't suggest anything else. By then she was more than ready to go home.

He dropped her at her front door and left, after thanking her for going along with him. Caryn could barely muster a smile as she thanked him for the day and went inside, collapsing against her door.

"All the man does is eat," she muttered, placing her hand against her too-full tummy. "Why can't he understand I feel better when I eat light in the evening?" Feeling the need to do something, she ran upstairs in search of her swimsuit.

Sam was trying to decide where to put his new lamp when he noticed Caryn, wearing a sweatshirt and pants and carrying a large towel, walking toward the swimming pool.

"She's the perfect example of an exercise nut," he muttered, turning away to his task.

A little over an hour later, when Sam walked over to the draperies to draw them shut, he realized Caryn's outside light was still on. He remembered her once telling him she enjoyed using the complex pool and how she left her front light on while she was gone. Not believing she had forgotten to shut it off he stepped outside. When he stopped first at her place he didn't find her home. The closer he came to the pool the clearer he could hear the faint sounds of someone moving through the water. Quickening his step, he fumbled for the key needed to unlock the gate and entered the fenced area to find Caryn swimming laps with barely a pause at each end. He wasn't sure why, but he sensed she hadn't stopped once since she'd started, and that made him furious.

"What the hell do you think you're doing?" he shouted when she reached his end of the pool.

Caryn paused. She grabbed hold of the coping and shook the water from her face.

"Last I heard this was called swimming." Her mild tone didn't soothe his burgeoning temper.

"And I suppose you've been swimming laps the entire hour you've been out here?" Sam wasn't sure exactly why he was angry with her, but he wasn't about to question it. "What are you trying to do, work off your dinner? If you hadn't wanted something so heavy all you had to do was say something. I'm not deaf, you know." He reached down, grasped her wrists and hauled her out of the water. Spying her beach towel on a nearby chaise longue, he picked it up and draped it around her shoulders. "Don't you realize how cold it is out here? You could catch pneumonia with a stunt like that."

"Sam, the pool is heated, I swim here on a regular basis, and I haven't caught so much as a stopped-up nose," she said patiently, as if speaking to a small child. "If I'm not worried, why are you?"

"Because against my better judgment I happen to care for you!" he shouted, waving his arms around.

Caryn's eyes widened fractionally. Otherwise, she gave no hint of her thoughts. "Don't complicate matters, Sam," she said coolly. "We're becoming good friends. Let that be enough."

Sam threw back his head and laughed, although it was apparent he didn't find her words amusing. "This is rich. I finally get the nerve to tell you how I feel, and you act as if I said you have good teeth. Caryn Richards, you're a difficult lady to figure out."

She leaned over, drying her shoulders and legs. Why couldn't he understand that she didn't dare feel anything for anyone? "Look Sam, my work has always come first. I don't have time for complications."

"Complications?" he repeated. "Okay, let's see if this complication will get to you." Uncaring that she was still wet and smelled more of heavy chlorine than perfume, he pulled her against him and kissed her deeply.

Caryn had no time to think as Sam's mouth moved over hers with alarming ease, his tongue easily gaining entrance to her mouth. She didn't think of resisting, only winding her arms around his neck and flowing with it. If there was any chill in the night air she didn't feel it between the warmth of Sam's body and the heat of his kiss.

When he finally released her he stood back, his mouth curved into a faint smile of satisfaction as he studied her wildly flushed face. He was certain he looked just as disheveled as Caryn, since her hands had been in his hair during their kiss. He could still taste her mouth on his.

Caryn stood on unsteady feet struggling to regain her harried senses as she stared at him wild-eyed. Finally regaining her senses, she lashed out. Sam had no time to react as Caryn's hand connected with his cheek.

"You idiot!" she shouted, stalking over to the chaise and gathering up her clothes. Not bothering to put them on, she left the pool area. "The last thing I need is complications. Can't you understand that? If that's what you want, try someone else and leave me the hell alone!" She walked out, slamming the gate behind her with a resounding metallic clank.

Sam took several deep breaths, still trying to figure out his own clamoring feelings. He looked down, saw the damp imprint of Caryn's body on his clothing, and chuckled.

"If she'd just relax a little she could turn out to be a great kisser," he murmured as he walked away.

Chapter Eight

"What is he trying to do to me?" Caryn muttered, walking back and forth across the length of her living room, the folds of her dusky-peach robe swishing around her bare legs. When she'd reached home she'd taken a quick shower and wrapped her damp tresses in a towel. But all the time she'd stood under the hot rushing water she couldn't block out the memory of Sam's anger when he'd found her at the pool, and especially, she couldn't forget his kiss.

Even as she paced the living room she couldn't erase the feeling of his mouth on hers, the way it moved so warmly over her lips and the brief touch of his tongue.

"No!" She swept her hand through the air as if to banish the image so easily.

She halted abruptly and breathed deeply, staring into space but seeing nothing. Finally convinced she had returned to normal, she ascended the stairs to the loft where she kept her drawing board.

She sat down with a clean sheet of paper in front of her and selected a new piece of charcoal to begin her new sketch. With her mind's eye picturing the scene of children playing in the nearby park, she began drawing with swift, sure strokes. She could still remember the day. She had gone for a long run one morning and had passed the park where several children played among swings, monkey bars, a jungle gym and a slide. Two little girls were trying to see who could swing the highest. When she saw that scene she knew it was what she wanted to draw for Jodi's birthday present.

This was the first evening in a while she had been able to sit down and draw. Still picturing the scene in her mind, she worked for the next hour and a half, thinking of the little girls on the swings and the boys vying for the monkey bars. When her aching shoulders finally intruded, jerking her back to the present, she relaxed with a sigh of relief to view her work.

Her smile slipped and her eyes darkened with something akin to horror when she realized she hadn't drawn the children after all, but had drawn several facial sketches of Sam. Some of him smiling, some portraying his devilish amusement, and one, the one that stunned her the most, with his eyes dark and expression the way he looked just before he'd kissed her. She swore under her breath and tore the paper from the board and crumpled it up, tossing it in the wastebasket. Realizing any further work was pointless, she stood up and headed for her bedroom with the hope that sleep would come swiftly.

SAM THOUGHT about their kiss, too, but in a different way. He couldn't have explained why he had done it, just that looking at Caryn, so natural and beautiful even wet, had prompted him to touch her.

"You're crazy, buddy," he told himself, staring down into his drink. "She wants nothing to do with you. She's let you know that enough times. So why do you beat your head against a wall trying to get her to notice you?''

Stretched out on the couch, his glass cradled between his palms resting on his chest, he thought long and hard over the past events regarding the magazine. He knew there was a key there. All he had to do was find it—hopefully, soon. Then neither he nor Caryn would have to see each other again, which he was wryly certain would cheer her immensely.

It was past midnight when he went up to bed. When he pulled the draperies shut he noticed the upstairs light on across the way.

''Working late gets you nothing but an ulcer, princess,'' he told the light. ''But I guess that's your idea of fun. And that's all that matters to you, isn't it?''

Sam stripped off his clothing, took a brief shower and settled himself in bed with the latest Tom Clancy book. Before he turned the light out more than an hour later he couldn't resist a peek out the window. Caryn's light was still on. He frowned. He knew he wouldn't be his best in the morning, with so little sleep, and wondered how she would cope, since she insisted how important eight hours' sleep were.

''No, I don't think I'll give up on you after all. Whether you care to admit it or not you need someone like me to lighten up your life.'' By the time he turned off the lamp and pulled the covers around him he was smiling in anticipation of brightening Caryn's days.

UNABLE TO SLEEP, and more than willing to blame Sam for her insomnia, she got up earlier than usual for her morning run, then dressed for work. When Caryn parked her car, the office garage was almost empty and the carpeted hallways of the building seemed to echo beneath her feet. She unlocked the door and entered the reception area, turning on the lights along the way. With each step she took, Caryn felt uneasy, as if she was being watched. Repressing the urge to run out, she continued down the hall to her office, keeping her ears tuned to the slightest noise, but all she heard was the faint hum of air-conditioning. She stopped at each office, turning on the light and looking around, but found nothing amiss. She felt too uneasy to enter for a more thorough check. When she reached her office, she found the door closed. It was never closed and that bothered her the most. She reached out her hand to turn the knob and swiftly drew it back as if the knob had emitted an electrical charge.

"Hello?" Pat's unsure voice sounded from the front.

"Back here," Caryn called out. "I see I'm not the only one who decided to come in early."

"I wanted to photocopy those reports before everyone got in," the secretary explained. "When I found the doors unlocked and the lights on I admit I felt a little uneasy. I almost called Security. Actually, I felt the way you look right now. What's wrong?"

She shook her head. "I'm not sure, but I have a bad feeling about this. But if you ever walk in and find the offices this way don't even wait, go ahead and call Security. I'd rather have a false alarm than another incident."

Pat looked past her. "Your door is never closed."

"I know."

Both women fell back a couple steps.

"Would you like me to call Sam and have him check this out?" Pat moved toward her desk.

"No!" Caryn said sharply. "We're both adults and we're probably allowing our imaginations to run away with us for nothing." She pulled her shoulders back and moved forward to grasp the doorknob with her hand before she lost her courage. Taking a deep breath she turned the knob and pushed the door open a crack. She looked around but found nothing suspicious lurking.

"Nothing here," she said, stepping inside, pushing the door open further. "Augh!" she shrieked when a wall of water splashed down around her.

"Caryn!" Pat screamed, running forward and viewing her boss, now soaked with what looked like dirty soapy water. "Are you all right?"

Caryn viewed herself with dismay. "This is disgusting," she moaned.

Pat disappeared and returned with a roll of paper towels, tearing them off several sheets at a time and handing them to Caryn, who wiped her face clean of the grimy water. She didn't bother trying to wipe her dress as she studied the ruined silk fabric.

"This dress was brand new," she grumbled. "It isn't even paid for yet."

"I don't think the store will take it back now," Pat said, attempting levity and failing miserably. Her faint smile disappeared under her boss's glare. "Sorry."

"I can't believe this." Caryn slipped off her suede shoes, looking at their drenched appearance with sorrow. "I'm going home to shower and change. Would you please call Maintenance and have them clean this mess up." She walked barefoot down the hallway, praying she wouldn't run into anyone she knew on her way down to the garage.

When she returned to the office ninety minutes later she found the maintenance crew wiping down the door and using an industrial vacuum to dry the carpet. Sam stood off to one side talking to a man writing in a notebook. Both men looked up when Caryn appeared.

"I understand you had quite a greeting earlier," Sam said. "Caryn, this is Lieutenant Kendall from the police department. Lieutenant, Caryn Richards, editor-in-chief of *Simple Fitness*."

The other man nodded. "We wished your maintenance men hadn't been so prompt, Ms. Richards, or that we had been called first."

"Since no one was hurt I didn't see any reason to call the police." She shot Sam an angry glare. "It was nothing more than a practical joke."

"Just like all the others were?" the police detective asked dryly, noting her start of surprise. "Oh, yes, we now know everything. You should have called sooner."

"That was up to Mr. Gregory and he saw it differently. He prefers keeping, and solving, company problems in-house. That's why we have our own security force." She flashed an acid-sweet smile at Sam.

"He'll change his mind now." Sam handed her a sheet of paper. "These are all over the street and circulating throughout the building."

Caryn read the crudely printed words and felt her anger mounting with every passing second.

"So our staff is nothing more than bimbos run by someone with a much more graphic description," she said tautly. "Right now nothing surprises me. So, Lieutenant Kendall, if you think you can do a better job than Mr. Russell here, who has done zip in the process, you have my blessing. I'm sick and tired of all this.'' She handed the paper back to the policeman. ''Gentlemen.'' She passed them by and entered her office, now free of the workmen, and slammed the door behind her.

Sam moved toward the door, but Pat's voice stopped him. ''I wouldn't if I were you,'' she advised. ''When Caryn's in that kind of mood it's safer to stay out of her way until she cools off.''

''Miss, we have some very nasty malicious mischief going on that could turn dangerous if we don't catch the person in time. If your boss knows anything at all that could help us she'll have to put aside any personal feelings and talk to me,'' the lieutenant insisted.

Pat shook her head. ''She came in this morning only to get doused with a bucket of very cold, dirty and soapy water, which ruined a brand-new outfit and shoes, not to mention her good mood. Give her some time and she'll talk to you. All right?''

He nodded, reluctant to leave but aware the secretary wasn't going to allow him access to her boss without a battle.

''I'll be back this afternoon around one-thirty. Make sure Ms. Richards is in the mood to talk to me then,'' were his parting words.

Sam remained behind. He stood in front of Pat's desk, leaning over and bracing his hands on the polished surface.

''I'd hazard a guess that the person behind this is after Caryn, not necessarily the magazine,'' he commented.

''I wouldn't tell her that if I were you,'' she suggested. ''Trust me. I've seen her in this mood and she doesn't like to talk to anyone who looks remotely human. And since you brought in the police you're going to be even further down her list. Your chances of seeing the boss lady outside the elevator are nil."

Sam nodded as he straightened up. "No problem. She'll talk to me when the time is right. See you later."

"I DON'T INTEND to bite anyone," Caryn informed her secretary when Pat crept in with several letters requiring her signature. "Correction—not anyone in this office."

Pat allowed herself a smile. "I don't think Sam would mind your nibbling on him."

Caryn's face reddened, as she thought of their kiss the night before. "Why did you call him?" she asked crisply.

"Because this is all getting out of hand," she replied bluntly. "Caryn, what if it hadn't been water in that bucket? What if it had been something harmful? I think Sam is right—this person has a personal vendetta against you. First the air horn, now this. Even you admitted you were wary when you first entered the offices this morning, and you didn't want to open your door. Oh, you tried to look brave, but I know you too well. Deep down you were afraid." Her face showed concern. "Sam had to know, Caryn, no matter what your personal feelings for the man are."

"I have no personal feelings for him."

Pat studied Caryn's set features but said nothing. She waited for her boss to sign the correspondence and picked up the letters. "I'll get these out," she murmured, leaving the office.

Left alone, Caryn covered her face with her hands as Pat's words rang in her ears. She was right. Caryn *had* been afraid to open the door, and when the first drops of water fell on her head she had feared it was something dangerous. But she'd bit her lips and kept the scream deep inside her. It wasn't until she had reached home that she let the fear escape. When she returned to the office she was her usual composed self, but she could feel the metallic taste fill her mouth.

"I am above it," she chanted softly. "I am above it. I am in charge. Nothing can hurt me." But all the time she murmured the words she felt as if she was lying to herself.

SAM AND LIEUTENANT KENDALL arrived in *Simple Fitness*'s offices at the same time. The detective looked at Sam with a slightly raised eyebrow.

"As head of Security I thought you wouldn't mind if I sat in," Sam said with a disarming smile.

"Something tells me I don't have a choice," the lieutenant said dryly, "although I have an idea that Ms. Richards can handle herself quite well on her own."

"Yes, she can, but Mr. Gregory would like to hear your point of view on this." Sam nodded and smiled at Lori as she buzzed Pat to inform her of her visitors.

"What about yours?"

"Let's have coffee after we're finished here," Sam suggested. "And I mean the real stuff. All they serve here is decaffeinated. I don't know about you, but it does nothing for me. I'll tell you my feelings then."

The other man nodded. "All right."

Caryn was the picture of a gracious hostess when the two men were ushered into her office. She led them over to the couch and chairs. Her smile was brittle when she viewed Sam.

"I didn't know you had joined the police force."

"Just here on behalf of the company, Ms. Richards."

He looked and sounded so affable it was enough to send Caryn screaming into the streets. She resisted the urge to grind her teeth and, with a pleasant smile, offered the men coffee. They glanced at each other and politely declined.

"Now, Ms. Richards—" Lieutenant Kendall opened a small leather-bound notebook "—I understand these pranks have been going on for some time. Including one where someone blew an air horn into the phone when you answered a call."

"That's correct." Now Caryn was all business. "More like malicious mischief than anything. Something Mr. Russell should have taken care of easily." Her eyes shot white-hot daggers at her subject. "It's a shame he had to call you in for something so minor."

"This is nothing minor, Ms. Richards," the detective said gravely. "In fact, I'd hazard a guess that whoever is behind this is after you personally."

Her forehead wrinkled. "Me, why?"

"Many reasons. Perhaps someone tried a product you endorsed and was hurt by it. Instead of blaming the product or even themselves, they prefer taking it out on you. A disgruntled past employee. Everyone has enemies if they care to look hard enough for them."

"The magazine doesn't endorse products, merely rates them against others, and I don't usually have anything to do with it," she protested.

"Someone that unbalanced doesn't care. They only want someone to punish," he explained.

Caryn's face didn't betray her feelings. She had to admit she hadn't thought of the person being emotionally unstable. She just thought it was someone out to get the magazine.

"What you're trying to say is that the next time I could be hurt," she spoke woodenly, feeling the fear rise within her.

"Maybe, maybe not. From what Mr. Russell has said there's been no pattern of the incidents to give us any hints."

"Well, if you want information you'd be better off talking to Mr. Russell, because he has everything there is to know about the past events," Caryn said tartly. "As far as I'm concerned no one is going to frighten me enough that I can't do my work. Now if you gentlemen will excuse me I have a magazine to put out." She stood up.

Recognizing her arrogant dismissal, the men stood. Lieutenant Kendall smiled and held out his hand.

"It's been a pleasure to meet you, Ms. Richards, and if there's anything I can do to help please don't hesitate to call on me."

"Just find this person so my staff won't worry every time they open a desk drawer, and I'll be happy. Good day."

When the two men reached the elevator, Lieutenant Kendall exhaled a breath of air. "Some lady," he commented, watching Sam punch the "up" button.

"Yeah, she sure is." His voice was tinged with pride.

The detective's eyes shifted to one side. "I'd say you have more than a professional interest in the lady."

"Yeah, I think I do," Sam admitted, as they entered the elevator car. "My problem is persuading her I'm not all that bad."

"And you plan to show her the error of her ways," he guessed.

Sam smiled. "Exactly." He pressed the button for his floor. "Now, for some real coffee, and I'll show you what I've come up with. Say, what do you think about guns that shoot rubber bands?"

CARYN DIDN'T SEE Sam for a few days although she heard his name among the staff as they mentioned having lunch or drinks with him. Even Pat commented they'd met one day.

"When I suggested he go out with other women I didn't expect him to try everyone," Caryn grumbled, sifting through the file folders until she found the correct one.

"Who's trying everyone?"

She looked up, not wanting to appear pleased that Sam stood in her office doorway. "What do you want?"

"Now that's a loaded question if I ever heard one." He walked in without waiting for an invitation and plunked down in a chair. "Basically I'm here to tell you that the list has narrowed greatly and hopefully we'll soon come up with the vandal. Doesn't that make you happy enough to have dinner with me tonight?"

"No."

"Drinks?"

"No."

He nodded as if understanding why she was so curt with him. "A glass of warm milk at bedtime, then?"

Before she could retort to his outrageous suggestion, Tami ran into the office.

"Caryn, did you find it? Oh, hi, Sam," she greeted him with a warm smile. "If you're not busy, Caryn, why don't you come into the studio and watch? We're setting up a shoot for our make-over."

"I'd like to. Sam was just leaving."

He turned to Caryn and smiled, his eyes glittering with a purpose she didn't want to read. "Now, Caryn, I don't recall saying that," he chided, standing up. "All I remember discussing with you was the merits of warm milk at bedtime."

Tami choked and rapidly turned away before her boss saw and heard laughter.

Stiff with anger, Caryn walked down the hallway to the studio with ground-eating strides, uncaring whom she left behind. When they entered the room she turned to Sam, the fury on her face silencing any comment he might have been ready to make.

"If you make one noise, I don't care if it's a cough, I will personally throw you out of here," she threatened in a low voice. "Do you understand?"

"I love it when you talk tough," he cooed.

Caryn opened her mouth prepared to scream with outrage, but Jay, unaware of the tension between the couple, mercifully intervened. She stood back, inwardly appalled by her feelings. While she might have lost her temper in the past she never lost control the way she did with Sam. It upset her a great deal, and she drew deeply on her inner reserves to rebuild the slowly crumbling wall she felt better behind.

"Caryn, great, you're here. What do you think of our new star?" Jay held his hand out, gesturing at a young woman dressed in a simple black dress with a bright red belt, standing next to a life-size poster of herself at a much heavier stage.

"Sharon, you look wonderful." All traces of her earlier anger were gone as Caryn greeted the young woman with the sincere compliment. "How did the weigh-in go?"

She blushed. "Only two pounds, but Lee told me not to worry because it will get harder the closer I get to my goal. Still, I see what I looked like in the beginning and I certainly can't complain." She wrinkled her nose at her picture.

Sam stood back, taking in the difference between the picture and the woman now. He would guess she had lost more than fifty pounds, her hair was restyled and her makeup artfully applied.

"We do two make-overs a year," Jodi said quietly, moving to stand beside him. "Sharon was chosen from about two hundred applicants because she wrote the most beautiful letter. She said she didn't want to lose weight just because she'd never gone out with men or because she wants to be popular, but because she felt it was time to find her real self, but she was afraid she might need some help. We called her in and liked her immediately. She's done well with her diet and exercise program, and every month we review her progress. We're also here if she has any problems in-between. She's even started dating recently."

"Quite a change," Sam commented.

"Even in her outlook on life," Lee said, stepping in. "She told me she always had a sort of a crush on a guy in her office, but she knew he wouldn't notice her. He asked her out a week ago and she very bluntly asked him why he hadn't asked her before. He told her he hadn't really noticed her until she lost weight. She then explained to him that she's really the same person, only thinner, and turned down the date. I have to give her credit. She's got a good head on her shoulders, and I'll be very surprised if she ends up putting the weight back on when this is all over.''

Sam stood in the background watching Jay put Sharon through a variety of poses, with the poster of her old self and without. He also watched Caryn talk to her, looking more at ease than he had seen her in a long while. When did he notice her as more than a co-worker? Of course, seeing her in the maillot the night before had answered any questions he might have had about her figure. He could understand why a woman would work so hard to keep a beautiful shape like that.

''She still needs to work on her kissing technique. I guess I better keep myself available,'' he said under his breath, watching her from across the room.

Chapter Nine

Caryn was dreaming about bells. Her sleep-filled mind was certain they were the kind of bells that rang on Sunday mornings. No, she protested, more like—like, her mind refused to think further as it tried to drift back to sleep, but wasn't allowed to as the bells continued ringing. As she returned to the land of the living she knew where the bells were coming from.

She sat up, pushing her hair away from her face as she listened to the incessant ringing, as if someone was leaning on her door bell.

"This is not fair," she groaned, blindly reaching for her robe and trying to slip it on. She stumbled downstairs, groping for the light along the way. "This better be good." She peered through the peephole, stepped back for a second then leaned forward to look again. "Oh, no."

"Come on, Caryn, I know you're up. I saw the light. I'm freezing out here."

She unlocked the dead bolt and threw open the door. "Do you know what time it is?" She wrapped her robe more tightly around her.

Sam glanced at his watch. "Not even one o'clock."

Caryn raised her eyes heavenward. "Not even one o'clock, he says. One o'clock in the morning, I'd like to add. What are you doing here?"

"My TV is acting up and *The Mole People* is coming on at one. I even brought the popcorn." He held up the large bowl he was holding in his hands as if he considered this the ultimate bribe.

She resisted the urge to let out a good healthy scream. "You got me up at one o'clock in the morning to watch a movie?"

"You can go back to bed if you want," he assured her with that endearing manner Caryn was finding more difficult to resist every time she saw him. "I'll keep the volume down low so it won't disturb you, although I wouldn't mind if you wanted to watch it with me. It's a really good film."

"How kind of you." Her sarcasm was blithely ignored. She knew when she was beat. She stepped back and gestured with her hand for Sam to enter. "I should know better," she muttered, following him into the living room and watching him turn on the television set and find the correct channel. Once he was settled on the couch, she curled up in the adjoining chair with the folds of her robe draped around her bare feet. "I must be crazy to go along with this. I shouldn't have even allowed you inside the house."

"You won't be able to get any popcorn if you're seated so far away," Sam told her, sprawling back on the couch. He had just started to prop his feet on the coffee table when he saw her censuring glance and quickly lowered them. "Sorry."

"Take your shoes off first," she advised sagely.

Smiling at her, he did just that. "I really appreciate this, Caryn. This is one of my favorite movies and I never miss it when it's on—even though I have it on tape."

"You must be a B-movie fan."

He nodded. "B horror movies. They had some real good ones come out in the fifties." His attention was diverted when the credits rolled. "I mean, look at the cast."

"Hugh Beaumont is in this? He played Ward Cleaver." Caryn was incredulous.

"Everyone has to get a start somewhere. After all, Clint Eastwood had a small role in *Revenge of the Creature* and Steve McQueen starred in *The Blob*." Sam appropriated one of the throw pillows on the couch and slid it behind his head.

As she watched the unrealistic plot unfold she couldn't help but become fascinated at the idea of people living beneath the earth with hideous monsters as their slaves. Before too long Caryn moved to the couch and nibbled on Sam's popcorn. While she might not have been completely aware of what she was doing, Sam was. Even though Caryn had gotten up once to turn up the heat, the air was still chilly and she moved closer to him for warmth.

"Do you notice how these fantasy kingdoms are always destroyed by an earthquake, or the sea overtakes their defenses, killing all the people except the heroine whom the hero has carried off to live in his own world?" she mused, when the ending credits rolled.

Sam pick up Caryn's *TV Guide*. "If you're not tired, *Monster on Campus* is on next," he suggested.

"You weren't kidding. You do like these," she groaned.

"John Agar, Troy Donahue. Oh, that's right, you hold a secret lust for Pee-wee Herman. I'm afraid he's not in this one."

Caryn chuckled. "Actually I'm not tired now, although I was ready to shoot you when you first showed up on my doorstep."

Sam studied her face. "You're not mad at me anymore?"

"I think you're safe for the time being."

He looked smug. "People tend to forgive me easily. Probably because I tend to grow on them."

"Mold has a tendency to do that, too. Luckily I've discovered an excellent cleanser to get rid of it."

He winced. "And here I thought I had you all softened up."

Caryn narrowed her eyes, looking at him suspiciously. "All softened up for what? I've already let you come in and watch your movie, haven't I?"

Sam leaned over. "Ah, but there's another important ritual to watching a movie other than eating popcorn," he murmured.

Her breath caught in her throat as she easily figured out his meaning. This time she had no intention of hitting him or drawing away, and she tried to blame her decision on the late hour. "Such as?" Her voice came out husky and inviting.

"Oh, something like this." His lips feathered over hers in the lightest of touches that left her wanting more. "And this." His tongue lightly touched the center of her lips and drifted over to one side. "And most importantly, this." His mouth covered hers fully, his touch stronger and more insistent as he coaxed her lips apart.

Caryn could taste the salt and butter from the popcorn Sam had eaten as she relaxed under his searching mouth. When his hands lifted to cradle her jaw, her hands lifted to caress his fingers. When his mouth trailed a moist path along her face to drop butterfly kisses on each eyelid, her lips traced the sharp blade of his nose.

"No nose jokes, okay?" he whispered against her cheek.

"You have a fine nose, a strong nose," she whispered back, touching the tip with her tongue. "A spectacular nose."

"Some say there's some Indian way back in my family. Hence the nose." Sam folded her against him, holding her tightly, inhaling the floral scent of her hair. "Oh, Caryn, do you realize how good you feel against me?"

"You don't allow me to stay angry with you very long, do you?" She closed her eyes, relishing the warmth of his body against hers, the way he demanded little yet seemed to get so much. "How do you do it?"

"Pure chance, and because I have an ulterior motive in mind where you're concerned," he informed her, blowing lightly in her ear.

She shuddered under the warm breath and would have pulled away if he had allowed her. She couldn't stop the disappointment from flooding her body as the realization that he was like the others came to her. What was it about her that men felt they had to dominate? Resolve hardened her voice. "I see."

Sam easily read her thoughts and couldn't help chuckling. "No, I don't think you do. Because my intentions are to teach you how to play. We'll work on the rest of it when the time is right.''

Caryn drew back to look at him more fully. ''To play what?'' Her voice was tinged with suspicion.

His laughter rumbled deep in his chest. ''What a dirty mind you have. I'm talking about taking time to smell the flowers, go to the beach.''

''It's a bit chilly for sunbathing,'' she pointed out.

Sam shook his head, clucking under his tongue. ''So you wear a coat when we walk along the shore. Going to the beach doesn't mean swimming or surfing. It can also mean walks on the sand, barbecuing, huddling under blankets and necking like teenagers.''

''Now that sounds more like your unique style,'' Caryn said dryly, unconsciously snuggling down further in his arms.

Sam exhaled a long-suffering sigh. ''I can see my work is cut out for me.'' He dropped a kiss on her ear.

''Did you ever stop to think I might not agree to your program?'' Caryn asked mildly, tipping her head to one side.

''You will, because no matter how much you protest, deep down you know you need me as much as I need you.''

His simple declaration left her stunned.

''Sam, we were only kissing.'' She stumbled over the words.

His arched eyebrow silently asked if she could truthfully label what had just passed between them as only a kiss.

Caryn disentangled herself from his arms, pulling her robe tightly around her, unaware that her body language was telling him she was trying to hide her true feelings. "You know very well what I mean," she said crossly.

He leaned against the couch arm and crossed his arms in front of his chest. "Do I?"

"Sam, I am diagnosed as a type A personality, a workaholic. That means work comes first, second and third. Everything else goes in whatever order I feel it deserves," she stated baldly.

"Then I guess you'd put me as far down the list as possible and even then leave a few blank spaces in-between." He didn't appear to feel threatened by her statement. He wasn't about to tell her that he expected her to say just that.

Her smile said it all. "My work is very important to me. I've had to give up a lot to get where I am, and I don't intend to allow anything to interfere with it."

Sam nodded. "Sounds fair, but you don't have to work twenty-four hours a day, seven days a week," he pointed out. "There's no law that says you can't get away on the weekends to take in a movie, go on a picnic." He grinned wickedly. "Indulge in a day of decadence. Show the new guy in town a good time. Take your choice."

Caryn held up her hand for silence. "All right, you've made your point, but that doesn't mean I'm agreeing to any of your ideas."

"Then how about a trip to the zoo? Wander through the museums and soak up some culture?" he suggested.

The more she heard the more she felt her resolve weakening. "You don't give up, do you? I'm a hard-boiled businesswoman. Why would you want to bother with someone like me when you could see a woman whose train of thought relates to yours?"

Sam shook his head. "No, I can't afford to if I want to find out something. I like you, Caryn, and while you try to hide them you have a lot of beautiful qualities that any man would treasure." His icy blue eyes bored deep into hers. "All I ask is a chance."

Oh, Sam, if you only knew what you were asking, Caryn thought to herself. A faint smile curved her lips. "How can I resist such a humble request?"

He chuckled, looking more relaxed than he had in a while. "Lady, you don't make it easy for a guy, do you?"

"Of course not. I wouldn't be where I am today if I did." With a great show of formality she offered him her hand. "Shall we shake on it?"

Sam shook his head. "No, I think this kind of deal requires a different form of binding our agreement." Without another word he pulled her back into his arms for a kiss that had steam coming out of Caryn's ears. When he finally released her he had a broad grin on his face. "I knew with a little practice you'd turn into a great kisser."

Caryn placed her hands on his chest and pushed away from him. "It's a shame you're so shy and retiring," she snapped, standing up, then wishing she hadn't when she discovered her legs were just a bit shaky. Awareness of who was to blame didn't improve her frame of mind any. "Now, it's past three in the morning and my alarm goes off at five-thirty."

"Five-thirty!" Sam looked horrified. "Why so early?"

"Because I run three mornings a week and tomorrow is one of those days," she explained patiently.

"Change days and sleep in," he suggested.

"I don't believe in changing a good thing. In fact—" she tapped her forefinger against her bottom lip, looking speculative "perhaps you would like to go along?"

He shuddered as if she'd asked the unthinkable. "No thanks. That's not my style."

"Afraid you'll collapse before you've finished one lap?" she challenged.

"Yes," Sam said bluntly. "Don't bother trying to get to me via my ego because it won't work. I'm well aware of my weaknesses and they don't bother me one bit, but I will go along and cheer you on."

"It would be more fun if you participated. After all, if I'm willing to do something with you you should be only too willing to do something with me."

He sighed. "Such as running."

"I'll even take it slow and easy for you," Caryn assured him.

"Why don't I feel comfortable about this?" Sam muttered, rising to his feet. "Okay, I'll be back here at quarter of six. Unless you're willing to let me spend the night here, then I'd easily be ready at five-thirty?" He looked hopeful, but she quickly quashed that idea.

"The couch isn't comfortable for sleeping, and since you live so close by I wouldn't worry about your falling asleep before you reached your home." Caryn smiled brightly, beginning to enjoy herself.

"You never can tell," Sam told her as he headed for the front door. "A couple of steps and I could fall right over. Oh well, thanks for the use of your TV."

"You're welcome. Just don't ever do it again."

"WHEN I BOUGHT these sneakers I never realized I'd actually use them for what they were intended for,"

Sam panted, certain every step he was taking would be his last.

Caryn turned around, running backward along the high-school track she had brought Sam to. "Keep your arms closer to your body," she instructed. "Breathe more slowly. You keep up that way, you'll end up hyperventilating."

"I breathe any more slowly and I'll die. Okay, that's it." He skidded to an abrupt stop and bent over, bracing his hands on his knees as he struggled to catch his breath. "You've proved your point. You're in much better physical shape than I am and you can outrun me. Does that make you happy?" he wheezed.

Caryn stopped, although she kept moving in place in order to keep her muscles warm. Suddenly she felt guilty for goading him into running with her. "Sam, this wasn't meant to be a contest. I just wanted to show you how much fun it can be."

He looked at her, disbelief etched on his sweat-streaked features. "Fun? You call it fun when you're running around a high-school track at the crack of dawn going nowhere in particular?"

Caryn bent over, grasping her ankles with her hands, stretching her leg muscles. "Don't you realize how much freedom running can give you? How good it makes you feel?" She tried to make him see how she felt. "When I'm out here I can free my mind, clear the cobwebs out of it."

Sam shook his head. "You run three times a week, attend exercise and ballet class whenever you can fit it in. When do you get time to work? In fact, where do you get the energy?" Maybe she felt good when she ran, but all he knew was there were a great many muscles in his body he wasn't aware of until now, he thought testily.

"If I didn't keep myself in shape I wouldn't be the proper image for the magazine," she retorted. "Everyone on the staff has their own physical-fitness routine."

"And I bet none of them are as tough as yours," he muttered. "I swear, Caryn, you make marine boot camp look like summer camp." He winced when he moved his leg. "Damn, that hurts."

"If you do some stretching exercises they'll help relieve any cramping," Caryn suggested, feeling even more guilty as she watched him move slowly. "I'm sorry, Sam."

He shook his head, laughing ruefully. "No, this was my own fault. I figured if I kept a slow pace I'd do all right, but instead I tried to keep up with you. I guess my male ego did step in, after all."

The moment Sam began to walk, Caryn hurried over and offered him her shoulder. "Here, lean on me if necessary," she offered. "What you really need is a hot bath and rubdown. In fact, I know where you can get both."

"Your place?" he asked hopefully.

She laughed and shook her head. "No, a health club nearby that I belong to."

Sam groaned as his body protested every movement he made. "It couldn't be open this early. Most people aren't alive at this hour."

"It opens at five." Caryn walked slowly, watching his face for any indication of pain.

"You mean there're other people in the world who actually get up this early to exercise just because they want to?" he moaned.

"A lot like to fit in a workout before they go to work," she explained. "Come on, only a few more steps to the car. Believe me, after some time in the Jacuzzi and a rubdown you'll feel like a new man."

"I'm going to hold you to that promise," Sam muttered. "By the way, you're sexy even wearing baggy sweatpants."

"Oh, Sam, will you never give up?"

"Now, DON'T YOU FEEL much better?" Caryn asked brightly a little over an hour later.

His expression was dark as he limped out to the car. "That place was pure Yuppieville. The other guys in the Jacuzzi could only talk about finance rates on condos, and I'm certain the masseur is a sadist at heart." He took the keys from Caryn's hand and unlocked the door for her. "I may be half-dead, but I can still drive."

Once they left the health club, Caryn half-turned in the seat. "I feel as if this is my fault. I admit I may have wanted to show you up a bit, but I didn't expect this."

"Chalk it up to one of our differences," he replied, turning right at the light. "You believe exercise is the most important part of life. I would rather enjoy life in other ways. We'll learn to blend them. And if I ever decide to try this kind of torture with you again I intend to take it slower."

"I'll make sure you do," Caryn vowed.

Sam hid his smile. As long as Caryn felt guilty enough to fuss over him a little he wasn't going to ignore such a wonderful opportunity.

When they reached the town house complex Caryn offered to drive them both in to work, but Sam declined, saying he had a meeting outside the building and wanted his car.

"One thing," he said before she walked away. "If you go in and find anything—I don't care if it's a strange hair on the carpet—you call me. If I'm not available, talk to Brian and have him come down, or call Lieutenant Kendall. Don't let yourself get doused again. Do you hear me?"

She smiled. "I promise."

"You're sounding too amiable, Caryn."

"I'm trying to act smart. I just don't want another dress ruined. The cleaners told me the last one was beyond hope. It would help if you could find this person soon."

"That I hope to do," he assured her. "Right now a couple of names stick out like sore thumbs. It's just a question of running them down. Luckily, Kendall doesn't mind our help in this. Most policemen would prefer to take over the investigation and throw out the civilians. Let's try and keep him on our side, all right?"

"I won't insult the man. I promise." She held her hand up as she vowed. "Just don't expect me to be too easygoing, or no one will recognize me."

Caryn didn't need to worry. When she entered her office a solemn-faced Pat handed her a pink message slip.

"He's called every ten minutes and said the minute you got in to call him back," she told her boss.

Caryn sighed as she switched her briefcase from one hand to the other as she read the word "urgent" written in red ink. "How did he sound?"

"Mad."

"Did he give any indication of how much he knows?"

"Everything."

Caryn nodded wearily as she entered her office. At that point she couldn't have cared less if a band of archers were waiting inside for her with their bows drawn. In fact she would have welcomed them. "Would you please bring me in some coffee, with hemlock for a chaser? I think I'm going to need it."

Caryn wasn't surprised that she was connected to her boss immediately.

"Good morning, Mr. Gregory," she said, greeting him with the deference she knew he preferred. "How are you today?"

"Not good," he growled. "What kind of hours do you keep out there? Do you realize how long I've been trying to get hold of you? I'm paying you good money to put out that magazine, and you seem to think you can flit in any time you want."

"I'm afraid you're forgetting the time difference, sir," she replied, resisting the urge to grind her teeth. "In fact we're all in here a bit earlier than usual today. It's only a quarter of eight." She sat stiffly as she heard the man rumble on about how work practices were when he began his first job. She bit back the urge to inform him that sweatshops were abolished years ago, not to mention the fact that there were many mornings she had been in the office at six. For a fleeting moment she thought of Sam's idea of work hours and wondered if they wouldn't be more humane.

"Why did you call the police in?" Mr. Gregory demanded to know. "If Russell can't do the job, I'll find someone who can."

"The police were called in because that bucket that merely splashed water on me could have fallen and hurt me badly," she said stiffly. "And we couldn't have me out of commission, could we? Mr. Russell thought it best to contact the police before something dangerous happened. They seem to think this person is after me and not necessarily the magazine."

"What the hell did you do to get someone so mad at you he has to attack the magazine, too?"

Caryn winced as the lionlike roar assaulted her ears. "The magazine is still a part of the problem, and we have no idea what I've done, although Mr. Russell feels he's very close to a solution," she stated.

"I bought that magazine because fitness and health is big money. When Marie couldn't do the job I got rid of her. You assured me you could manage it."

"And I have," she broke in, feeling her anger rise. "I took what was a mediocre magazine and, with a lot of sweat and hard work on my part, sent it to the top five in record time. Mr. Gregory, you have no idea what I gave up to accomplish this."

"You wanted the job," he stated baldly. "So don't give me that bull about sacrifices. My worry is, with the police involved, bad publicity can only follow. I don't want to see the sales figures falling. You hear me?"

"Loud and clear." Caryn stared blankly at the open doorway, not even seeing Pat standing there listening to every word.

"I'll be keeping an eye on you. Don't disappoint me." Without bothering with amenities he hung up.

Caryn replaced the receiver with great care.

Pat grimaced as she placed the coffee cup on the desk. "I gather he isn't happy that Sam has some solid leads?"

"You gather correctly," she sighed, looking at her calendar. "Naturally, I would have a staff meeting today."

"Dr. Milford is also coming in for the meeting to discuss those articles he's going to write for us," Pat explained.

"Oh, yes. All right." She glanced at her watch. "I have just enough time to drink this coffee and take a couple of deep breaths before the meeting."

"I'll make sure you aren't disturbed." Pat left, closing the door behind her.

Caryn leaned back in her chair, sipping the hot coffee.

"Oh, yes, Mr. Gregory, you have no idea what I've given up for this magazine," she whispered.

Chapter Ten

"She really knows where to hurt a guy," Sam muttered, his ears still ringing from his conversation with Mr. Gregory as he descended in the elevator to the floor of the magazine offices.

When Lori explained that Caryn was just finishing up a conference, he merely nodded and said he'd go back upstairs. He found Caryn standing in the hallway talking to a man who appeared to be in his early forties.

"I think a series of articles on the subject would be wonderful," she told the man. "And from what I hear it's happening more and more to older women, not just teenage girls. I like the idea of gearing some of the articles to the career woman."

"Let's not forget the young girls who believe too seriously in their baby fat," he replied grimly.

Caryn looked up and saw Sam, her lips warming in a smile. "Hi, there. Sam, come meet Dr. Milford. He has an eating-disorders clinic in Long Beach, and he's agreed to write a series of articles dealing with eating problems for us. Doctor, this is Sam Russell, head of Wes Com's security. Those offices are a few floors up."

"Doctor—" the two men shook hands "—I've noticed a lot of information has been given on the subject, between the books coming out, movies made for TV and talk shows. No offense, but what can you say that will be new?"

"Not much," the older man admitted. "The thing is, this disorder is so dangerous that enough can't be said about it."

"It is so sad what these girls do to themselves in hopes of making themselves perfect," Caryn interjected. "Tami and I visited the clinic a few weeks ago where we were able to meet and speak to a few of the patients. After that we toyed with doing an article on the clinic. We met with Dr. Milford, and after reading some of the articles he's written for medical journals we asked if he'd care to contribute to us."

"Anorexia and bulimia," Sam mused.

"More than that," the doctor told him. "Some bulimics also overexercise instead of purging, and anorexics completely forget what food is. So many die with complications or are left with serious health problems. Before, we used to see it mostly with teenagers. Now it's women in their twenties and thirties who are cropping up more and more."

"Why?"

"They figure it's easier than sticking to a diet, or pressures get to them. This way they figure they're in control."

"Why women would abuse their bodies like that is so sad," Caryn said again, softly, shifting her armload of file folders from one arm to the other. "If they could learn to stick to a good exercise program and a healthy diet they could indulge every so often without harming themselves."

The doctor smiled. "Unfortunately they don't see it that way, or something in their lives won't allow them to."

"Maybe you should talk to the man about your own crazy exercise program," Sam suggested to Caryn.

She shot him a warning glance. "Mine is perfectly acceptable, thank you. You're the one who needs to set one up before your body decides to punish you for all the liberties you take with it, and you suddenly wake up one morning with a paunch."

"This sounds like a long-standing argument between you two," Dr. Milford said with a chuckle. "If you'll excuse me I'll get back to my own work. It was nice meeting you, Mr. Russell. As for Caryn, I wouldn't worry. She looks like one of the healthiest women I've seen in a long time."

"Thank you for taking time out from your heavy schedule to come." Caryn offered him her hand and walked with him out to the lobby. When she returned to the conference-room doorway she found Sam gone, and then headed for her office where she found him comfortably ensconced in a chair, glancing through their latest issue.

"A person's coloring is attributed to the four seasons?" He looked skeptical as he tossed the magazine on her desk. "I don't know. I never thought of myself as a spring."

"For many women it's very helpful when they have to shop for clothing, because they'll choose colors that coordinate and will look very good on them." She sank into her chair. "Something tells me you're not here on a social call."

Sam's laughter was mirthless. "It wasn't enough that you tried to run me to death on the track during

the early-morning hours. Then you have me pounded
to death by a masseur. Oh no, you had to sic old man
Gregory on me. Thanks a lot. What are you going to
do for an encore?''

''He wanted information I felt you could give him
a great deal better than I could,'' Caryn said airily.
''Besides, why should I have all the fun chatting with
the man?''

Sam scowled and muttered dark words under his
breath.

''I beg your pardon?'' she asked sweetly, although
she had heard every word.

''I try to keep my language clean around women,
and you're rapidly changing that rule.'' He ran his
fingers through his hair, a sign of frustration.

''Caryn.'' Pat stopped short in the doorway. She
looked from one to another, a strange light in her eyes.
''Hi, Sam. You and your crew are going to join us this
Saturday for our football game and picnic, right
Caryn? After all, they are part of the family, so to
speak.''

''Sam isn't into sports. Correct, Sam?'' She turned
to him, her expression silently ordering him to de-
cline.

''Some sports I don't mind. In fact it sounds like a
lot of fun. I can't speak for everyone, but I'll tell my
staff about it and have someone get back to you for
the particulars. Since Caryn lives so close to me we can
go together.''

''I generally don't attend,'' she smugly informed
him. ''Especially when I have a lot of work to do, such
as I do this weekend.''

''But I'm sure she'll make an exception in the interest of the company,'' Pat cut in. ''Won't you, boss?''

"She will," Sam said confidently. "I'll make sure of it."

Pat positively beamed. "I know you will."

"Just whose side are you on?" Caryn demanded, looking incredulously at her secretary.

"Everyone's." After having the last word she returned to her desk.

"Don't worry, Caryn. You can outdo me at football, too," he assured her. "In fact if you play your cards right I might even let you tackle me." He pushed himself out of his chair. "Well, back to work. I've got a few things to check on this afternoon. The security system went crazy in the offices of that accounting firm on the sixth floor, and I've got to go out and talk to the company that installed it. They're trying to say it isn't their fault, and from what I can see the installation is all screwed up, causing the alarm malfunction."

"What happens?"

"The silent alarm goes off every half hour. We finally shut it down."

"Why don't we have anything like that up here? I would think that would stop the intruder. Perhaps even catch him in the act, as long as we have a silent alarm that works," Caryn remarked.

Sam shook his head. "I don't think so, because I'm certain this last prank was an inside job. Now, if I can just prove it. I've checked out every member of the maintenance crew and their references are impeccable, but I still think that's where I'll find answers."

"What you are saying is you don't have the slightest clue or lead, but you're positive you can find our prankster among the maintenance crew. Sam, I hate to tell you this, but that kind of thinking belongs on TV."

"Maybe so, but it's worked for me in the past, so I never ignore a hunch. Now don't work too hard. I want you in great shape for this weekend." With a jaunty salute he sauntered out.

"Justifiable homicide would work very well here," Caryn murmured, staring down at her desk.

"Oh, come on, Caryn, he's an absolute darling and you know it," Pat protested, walking inside. "Why don't you break down and give him a chance? It's more than obvious he wouldn't mind getting to know you better."

Caryn thought of the day they spent so companionably at the flea market and the night watching an old film, not to mention indulging in some excellent kissing, of which even the thought left her tingling. She hated to admit to herself that Sam was on her mind more and more. She wondered what had happened to her so-called rational self that saw men as nothing more than escorts. No, she had never been that harsh, had she?

"Sam has no trouble getting what he wants," she murmured. "He's arrogant enough for ten people."

"Then he's more than perfect for you," Pat insisted. "Because it would take someone that strong-willed to put up with you." She grinned to take the sting out of her words. "Let Sam take you to the picnic. Besides, he said you can get even with him at football, right? So, do it if it will make you feel better."

"Don't tempt me."

"THE MAN KNOWS HOW to play football," Jodi murmured, sitting cross-legged on the grass next to Caryn. "Look at him run."

"Look at his nice buns," Tami mused from Caryn's other side. "Um, very nice, if I do say so myself. The man really knows how to wear jeans—tight and worn. Caryn, you are so lucky to have him snapping at your heels."

Caryn looked from one to the other. "You two are unbelievable. Especially you, Tami. Brian has been hanging on to your every word since he got here."

"I'm not complaining. He's a really nice guy," she agreed. "In fact none of Sam's staff is nothing to sneeze at. Hmm, wouldn't that be something if we all got together with his male agents?"

"The idea sounds too much like a business merger," Jodi said. "Besides, I'm quite happy with my Ted." Her face glowed as she watched one of the men running across the grassy area designated as their playing field.

"Jodi in love is almost nauseating," Tami confided to Caryn. "Next thing we know we'll have to throw a wedding shower, and she'll walk around all starry-eyed. Just give me a good case of healthy lust any time. It saves a lot of wear and tear on the heart."

"In this day and age that idea isn't too healthy," Caryn told her, keeping her eyes on Sam. As if realizing she was watching him he glanced over once and waved. Tami was right—his rear view was just as good as his front. "How does he do it if he hates exercise so much?" she asked herself under her breath.

"That's why I'm so picky about my men." Tami leaned back, bracing herself on her hands. "Who knows, if Brian plays his cards right . . ." She lifted an eyebrow suggestively.

"It's a shame you're so shy and retiring, Tami," Jodi teased. "Not to mention unaware of your sex appeal."

She flipped her shiny black hair behind her shoulder. "Hey, hon, whatever works."

"It's the exotic look," Janna chipped in, sitting down beside Tami. "It gets the guys every time. They practically fall all over themselves when they meet her. In fact, it's downright sickening."

"Wrong, there're a few who tend to remain upright without any problem, Sam being one of them." Tami slanted Caryn a teasing look. "I think our boss lady has him all tied up in a nice and neat package."

"Sam is a free agent in every way possible," Caryn said stiffly, staring straight ahead, disconcerted to find her eyes following Sam's every move and hating herself for it. His baseball shirt was streaked with grass stains, his hair windblown, and he looked even more appealing. She groaned when Jodi's boyfriend tackled him. "I can't believe we're sitting here watching them as if this is some kind of ritual. The men run and tackle one another while the women sit on the sidelines watching them with adoring eyes. Why aren't we out there?"

The others looked at her with surprise.

"That's usually my line," Tami said. "Although I have an idea that if we suggest it they just might agree. Have you noticed everybody is huffing and puffing a bit more than usual?"

"That's because some of us have left the big three-oh behind, and others are staring it in the face," Pat moaned. "Therefore we tend to huff and puff more

and notice other nasties, such as gray hair and wrin-
kles."

"That's it." Ted, a balding bank-loan officer, collapsed on the grass beside Jodi. "I'm dead."

"It was probably that third hot dog that did you
in," she said.

"Nah, more like those brownies you brought." He
laughed and ducked when Jodi began playfully hitting him around the shoulders.

"Okay, ladies, your turn," Sam panted, dropping
to his knees in front of Caryn. "Go for it."

"I beg your pardon?" she asked haughtily.

"It isn't fair that we have all the fun," he insisted,
using the hem of his T-shirt to dry his sweaty face.
"So, we're willing to sit here and watch you play."

"Sounds fair," Brian agreed, walking up and tossing the football to Caryn. "Go for it."

She turned to the other women sprawled around
her. "What do you think?"

"Why not?" Lee laughed. "If nothing else, we can
show them how the game *really* should be played."

Amid good-natured jeers from the men, the women
ran out to the field and chose up sides, with Caryn and
Tami voted to be opposing captains.

"Do we honestly know how to play this game?"
Caryn asked the others. "What I'm saying is, how
many of you watch Monday Night Football?"

A majority confessed they did watch the game, not
for love of the sport but to watch the players. In the
end the women decided their game would be executed
more for fun than sport.

Caryn crouched over Lee who would be passing the
ball back to her.

Calling out "36-24-36," she added loudly. "Don't pass it back too hard. I don't want to break a nail."

The men on the sidelines roared with laughter, shouting their own form of encouragement.

"If you tumble, don't fall on your hands or you'll break one of your precious nails."

"And the ladies are lining up for the first down." One man imitated Howard Cossell.

"Think their makeup is sweat proof?"

When Tami intercepted the ball from Lori, she stopped in the middle of the play.

"You know I really like your hair that way. Who are you going to now?"

Lori kept up with the game. "Oh, this great guy on Melrose. He's a bit strange, but he gives the greatest haircuts." She stood there with her hand on her hip giving a blow-by-blow account of her last hair appointment.

Caryn was next, shrilly screaming that no one was allowed to tackle her because she didn't want any grass stains on her clothing.

"This is better than, 'Worst Moments in Football,'" Brian chuckled.

"At least they're prettier to look at." Sam watched Caryn, feeling a hunger build inside. Dressed in a dark gold sweatshirt, a pair of faded jeans and hair flying like a banner behind her, she looked more approachable than she had in a long time. He ached to hold her in his arms, to feel again the soft scented skin he knew her clothing hid. He watched her leap up to intercept Lee's throw then suddenly scream, dropping down to the ground and putting her hands to her face.

Sam was up and running in an instant, his heart pounding with fear.

"Let me in," he ordered, pushing his way through the circle of women surrounding Caryn, who now sat on the grass, her hands covering her face. He crouched down, gently taking hold of her hands. "Caryn, honey, let me look."

"It hurts so much," she sobbed in pain. "It was as if something bit me, but there aren't any bugs around."

"Caryn, come on, take your hands away from your face and let me see," he coaxed, carefully releasing her hold finger by finger. He cursed under his breath when he saw the ugly bruise already forming around her eye. He probed as carefully as possible, wincing each time she gasped, as if he also felt the pain. "This is not a bite."

"Sam." Brian passed something under his line of sight.

Sam looked down and saw a rock. "Are you trying to say this is what could have caused it?"

"Are you telling us this might have been done deliberately?" Tami demanded.

Brian turned it over. In bright red letters was painted "For Caryn."

"But why?" she cried, staring at the rock with shocked eyes. "Why is someone doing this to me?"

Sam assisted her to her feet. "Come on, I'm taking you to the hospital. I want your cheek and eye checked out by a doctor."

"No, I'm fine," she argued. "Please, I just want to go home and wash my face."

Lee stepped in. "Caryn you have to have it checked. For all you know your eye could be badly injured."

"Let Sam take you," Pat told her, coming up with a cool damp cloth for her to put against her cheek.

"Come on, honey, humor me just this once, okay?" Sam slipped his arm around Caryn's waist, guiding her across the grass toward the parking lot while the others stayed behind, stunned by the vicious attack.

"How could this happen?" Pat cried out. "Why would someone deliberately throw a rock at her and why didn't we notice anything?"

"Easy. We were concentrating on watching you ladies and naturally, had no idea something would happen away from the office, and certainly not something like this," Brain replied. "It's purely a hunch, but I'd say whoever did it is very skillful with a slingshot. The shot was too clean for someone to have just thrown it. Besides, it had to be done at some distance, so by the time we realized what happened he would have gotten away."

Tami wrapped her arms around her body as if she felt chilled. "This isn't fair," she murmured. "Caryn's never done anything to anyone, yet all this is happening. When it was happening to all of us, we just ignored it. But how can we forget this? What if that rock had hit her right in the eye? She could have been blinded."

"I'd say that if we ever catch this guy, he better hope he's kept far away from Sam, because he just might decide to kill him for this," Brian said.

"See, I told you everything was fine," Caryn informed Sam as they left the hospital emergency room three hours later. She groped for her sunglasses in her purse and slipped them on even though it had already grown dark.

"You're not a doctor." Sam inserted the key in the ignition and switched on the engine, allowing it to warm up before adjusting the heater. "Besides, I feel better hearing a member of the medical profession tell me you're all right."

"Yes, but Lieutenant Kendall isn't a doctor. Why did you have to call him?" She knew she probably sounded like a querulous child, but she didn't care. Her head hurt even with the medication the doctor had given her before she left. She didn't believe in taking too much medicine, but this was definitely the time to make an exception.

"Because this is part of everything else that has gone on. He wants to talk to everyone in the group to see if something out of the ordinary might have been noticed. I'm sorry to say so, but I doubt it. As for having you checked out. It was a good thing I did. Don't forget I was there when the doctor warned you that you might have blurred vision and headaches. Not to mention a beauty of a black eye."

"Terrific, and I have a meeting on Monday," she groaned, resting her head back on the seat.

"Don't worry, I'll be around to check on your blurred vision," he assured her. "And we're in luck. *The Brain from Planet Arous* and *Donovan's Brain* are on tonight."

"You know what? The doctor was right. I feel a killer headache coming on," Caryn moaned.

"I think I better stay with you to make sure you don't have any bouts of dizziness," he decided. "You shouldn't be alone."

"My headache has nothing to do with it. What I'm really saying is your choice of films is giving me a headache." She closed her eyes. "Sam, why would someone do this?"

"I don't know, but when I find the bastard he's going to wish he never heard of you or the magazine," he said grimly, taking great care to turn the corner, sensing her aching head wouldn't appreciate any abrupt turns. After he shifted gears, he reached over and grasped her hand lying limply in her lap and squeezed it before shifting gears again.

"Sam..." Caryn spoke in a low voice just before he turned into the complex.

"What, Caryn?"

"I don't want to be alone tonight."

He smiled. "Kinda hard for you to admit, wasn't it?"

It was several beats before she answered in a small voice, "Yes."

Sam parked his car in the garage and helped Caryn out, the two of them walking around the building toward her place. She frowned when she noticed lights burning brightly in the living room and kitchen.

She reached out and clutched his arm. "Sam, I didn't leave any lights on when I left."

He halted and looked at her face, pale except for the vividly colored bruise on her cheek. "You don't have a timer set to turn on the lights when it gets dark?"

"No."

"You should, but we'll get into that later." As they walked along, he kept a few steps ahead of her. After what had happened earlier, he felt the need for extreme caution. "Give me your keys and stay behind me. If there's anything out of the ordinary I want you to run like hell, do you understand?"

"Yes." Caryn handed her key ring over, the front-door key singled out. Sam kept her behind him as he unlocked the door and slowly pushed it open. After

her traumatic afternoon, Caryn could only stand behind him clutching his jacket.

"Caryn, why are you standing out there?" A tall
slim gray-haired man appeared at the entrance to the
living room. "And what happened to your face? I
certainly hope whomever you went three rounds with
looks worse than you."

Sam couldn't miss the way her body stiffened at the
man's greeting. He found he didn't like the way the
man spoke to her, as if the black eye and bruised cheek
could have been her fault. He sensed trouble.

"Sam, I would like you to meet my father, Gerald
Richards," Caryn said in a flat voice, all sparks of
emotion gone from her manner.

Chapter Eleven

"Good Lord, girl, have you no sense?" Gerald Richards looked at her with disgust, implying the injury was her fault.

"Gerry, she's been badly hurt," Lisa, Caryn's mother, said, putting a comforting arm around her daughter's shoulders.

Caryn winced, aware that Sam must have heard her father's remark as he left. After stilted introductions, Sam had explained the situation in a terse voice, bid Caryn a good-night and left. Had thrown her to the wolves was more like it.

"From what I can understand it is her fault," he gritted, turning to Caryn. "All the time you've yapped about your precious magazine you've never said someone might come gunning for you. And you thought sports were dangerous at times!"

Caryn could feel her headache pounding like a hundred drums. "So far no one has come gunning. Obviously it's someone who didn't like one of the articles." She tried to pass if off lightly, but found it difficult to do when all she wanted to do was lie down and block out the dull pain. "Look, I'm sorry, but while it's wonderful that you two decided to surprise me, I have a horrendous headache and I'd really like to go to bed.''

"A headache is forcing you to bed? Girl, you've gotten soft."

Ignoring the white spots dancing before her eyes, Caryn spun on her father. "Look, Dad, if I had been hit a bit closer I could have lost my eye. So I think I'm handling this pretty well, considering everything. And no matter how tough your football stars are I'm sure there've been times they've been hit with the ball and haven't felt so hot afterward. The problem is they're just too scared of you to say so! Now, I'm going to bed. Mom, you know where the sheets are.'' She kissed her mother on the cheek and walked up the stairs, holding on to the banister for fear of falling to her knees and refusing to do so in front of her father.

Foregoing a shower, Caryn took a quick sponge bath and pulled on a soft flannel nightgown. When she reentered her bedroom she found her mother sitting on the edge of the bed holding a mug in her hand.

"Oh, Mom, I'm sorry I snapped at you that way.''

The woman whose tawny hair matched Caryn's in every way except for the heavy silver threaded through it, and delicate features that echoed her daughter's, smiled. "Honey, you had every right. Now, come get into bed and let me brush the snarls out of your hair. I brought you some warm milk." She settled her daughter into bed and handed her the mug. "As for your father, I know you don't believe it, but he does love you."

"Then he has a hell of a way of showing it,'' she muttered, sipping the milk sprinkled with nutmeg, her mother's special touch. "Today just didn't turn out to be the way I'd planned it." she said ruefully, gingerly touching her bruised cheek.

"Sam Russell seems very nice," her mother said quietly, running the brush through Caryn's hair.

She closed her eyes, feeling very tired. "He is, although I'm positive Dad wouldn't like him at all. Sam's idea of exercise is walking to his car, and eating greens means putting relish on his hot dog."

Lisa smiled. "What about you?"

"Oh." Caryn's words were slurred. "Sam kinda grows on you, know what I mean?" Her mother grabbed the mug before it spilled and set it to one side. Caryn was fast asleep.

SAM WAS IMMERSED in his movie when the phone rang. Brian identified himself on the other end.

"I had the others search out the area very carefully, and Scott and I talked to a few people we saw. Oh, there were a couple of spots with the brush trampled, but no proof it had happened recently. What did the doctor say about Caryn?"

"She was lucky it didn't hit a bit more to the right or it could have injured her eye badly. She's also got a beauty of a black eye. I called Kendall, and he came down to take a report, which didn't please her at all. Luckily she wasn't in any shape to argue about it," he replied.

"I was going to try you over at Caryn's first since I figured you'd be there." There was a question in his words. "I guess it's a good thing I didn't call there."

"I had fully intended to be. We got back and found the lights on, which naturally sent her into a panic. It turned out her parents had shown up to surprise her," he said wearily. "Although after meeting her father I was sorely tempted to remain for her sake."

"As hard-nosed as she can be?"

"Caryn's a novice compared to this guy." He rubbed his forehead with his fingertips. "The minute he began yelling at her for her black eye as if it was her fault, I could feel the tension flowing into her body. I have an idea he's not her favorite person. Of course that lets me know I'm not her least-favorite person," he joked feebly.

"You know, Sam, this could be a warning telling us our time is running out." Brian's thoughts were parallel to his.

"I've been thinking that, too. As much as I hate to ruin the weekend, I'm going to call everyone for a meeting over here tomorrow morning at eleven. In fact, would you mind stopping by the office on your way over tomorrow and bringing the files? I want this creep stopped," he said grimly.

"Got it," Brian said promptly. "I'll be there."

Sam spent the next hour calling the rest of his staff and setting up the meeting. After being at the football game everyone was more than willing to give up the rest of their weekend to try to solve the case before further injury.

When he finished he went back to the living room and finished his movie, although he couldn't remember later what he saw. His thoughts were set on the woman sleeping soundly across the way.

"NOW I KNOW what a prizefighter looks like the morning after," Caryn moaned, staring into the bathroom mirror. The skin surrounding her left eye was all the colors of the rainbow, including a few new shades, and very tender to the touch. Digging through her makeup she found some pancake base and carefully touched it over the bruise. While it didn't cover it fully, the color was slightly diminished. Dressed in jeans and a soft mint-green sweater, her hair pulled up in a ponytail, she felt ready to face her father.

"It doesn't look all that bad," he pronounced, looking up from his coffee and waffles when she entered the kitchen.

"That's why they say makeup is pure magic," she said lightly, walking over to her mother and kissing her on the cheek. "Sorry I slept so late. I guess it was the pills the doctor gave me that knocked me out. Those waffles smell heavenly. Where's mine?"

Gerald looked at his daughter critically. "Maybe you should just settle for coffee. You've put on a couple of pounds, haven't you?"

"No, Dad, I haven't gained an ounce since the last time you saw me," she said tightly. "And I fully intend to have one of Mom's famous waffles loaded with butter and syrup."

Lisa shot her husband a warning look and ordered her daughter to sit down. "How's the headache?" she asked, pouring batter into the waffle iron.

"Better after I took one of the pills the doctor gave me." She sipped her coffee.

"Medication only slows you down," Gerald announced.

"Yes, but when you've got a headache that makes you think you have Big Ben standing inside your head, you're willing to have the slow reflexes." Caryn set her cup down and laced her fingers together, placing them on the table. "Look, Dad, we haven't agreed on anything since I changed my major in college. For once, can't we have a nice visit without arguing and upsetting Mom? Why don't you tell me how you think the team will do next year?'' She knew that was a safe subject that could keep her father talking for a long time. As he rambled on about his new star quarterback and plans for the next season, Caryn glanced out the window and noticed people walking into Sam's unit. "Now what?" she murmured.

Lisa followed her daughter's glance. "Anyone you know?" She was well aware of Caryn's penchant for not mixing with her neighbors.

"Sam lives over there and I'd say that's his entire staff." She sighed. "I have an idea he's called a meeting because of yesterday."

"You still haven't said why somebody would be after you." Gerald's voice had lost a bit of the hard edge it usually had.

"Probably because we don't know the exact reason. All we can figure out is someone has it in for me and the magazine because of an article written, either against the person directly, or they read it that way." Caryn shrugged. "The problem is narrowing it down, which is what Security has been doing."

"What does Mr. Gregory think of all this?" Lisa asked, placing a golden brown waffle in front of her daughter. Caryn could feel her stomach churning at the innocent mention of her boss's name, and the thought of eating the waffle was repugnant. "He isn't very happy about it," she murmured.

"I'm sure he isn't," her father retorted. "I suggest you get out of this while the getting is good, or before he puts the blame for this on you and gets rid of you."

Caryn cut her waffle into neat squares and lifted the first piece to her mouth. "I'll deal with that when the time comes."

Disgusted that she wasn't listening to what he was convinced was good advice, her father left the table and announced he was going for a walk.

"It never takes us long, does it?" Caryn sighed, after she heard the slam of the front door.

"That's because the two of you are so much alike." Lisa sat down across from her.

Caryn rolled her eyes. "Oh, please, Mom, don't insult me that way." She flushed as she realized how her words sounded. "Sorry. After all, he must have some good in him if you married him. Oops, I did it again, didn't I?"

Lisa chuckled. "Caryn, I'd be the first to agree that your father isn't one of the most flexible men around. In fact he's certainly one of the most stubborn, but he's always taken good care of his family."

"As long as it didn't interfere with a game or practice," Caryn muttered. "Don't you see, Mom? He's been angry with me ever since I changed my major to English. He couldn't understand why I didn't want to concentrate on my running until I reached the Olympics, or why I wouldn't end up coaching women's college sports. He may live and breathe sports, but I can't." She was pleading with her mother to understand. "I wanted more than to stay in training for the rest of my life and marry someone who was as focused as I was supposed to be."

"Is that why you still run several times a week and have the training schedule of an athlete?" Lisa asked gently. "When was the last time you touched your chalks?"

Caryn shrugged. "My work has kept me pretty busy, but I still draw when I have the time."

"What about Sam?"

"He works for the same company and our philosophies definitely don't mix."

Lisa smiled. "I'd say you'd be happy with that after your run-ins with your father." She picked up the dishes and walked over to the sink, then ran hot water over them.

Caryn looked across the walkway and wondered what was going on inside Sam's place. She suddenly wished he had been able to stay with her last night. She would even have put up with the horror movies to have him keep her company, instead of having another of the long-standing arguments with her father.

"While your father is walking off his breakfast and temper, would you like to do some shopping?" Lisa asked. "As much as you hate to admit it, your bathroom towels are a disgrace."

Caryn laughed. "I swear, Mom, the world could fall down around our ears and the first thing you would check is the state of the bathroom towels. All right, let me go up and get my purse. Let's see how much damage we can do to Dad's charge cards." She rubbed her hands together with expectant glee.

"I REALLY THINK Jerome Jenkins has something to do with this," Sam told the group. "The thing is, his secretary told us he's away on an extended cruise. In checking into his past record, we discovered he had to close down his spa when *Simple Fitness* ran an article that rated his the lowest, not to mention word of lawsuits. The man insisted that the magazine was to blame for his misfortunes. Using another name, he's currently putting out various exercise machines, advertised on television, and doing a booming business. We ordered someone to check it out. He also is starting up an exercise-clothing business under his wife's name. This guy has been very busy, but word is he was very bitter over the magazine's article on him. I didn't want Caryn to know about this until we had more solid facts."

"And just because he's on an extended cruise doesn't mean he couldn't have had everything mapped out ahead of time," Chad, one of the investigators, guessed.

Sam nodded as he poured himself another cup of coffee and helped himself to a blueberry danish, a contribution to their get-together. "Exactly."

"What I would like to know is how this person knew we were going to be out there yesterday," Barbara, one of the other investigators, said.

"Which brings me back to the idea of this being an inside job," Sam said. "Pat mentioned there was a memo tacked on their bulletin board for the past month. Anyone could have seen it."

The group nodded.

"And it would have been too easy to find some kind of clue yesterday," Brian said glumly.

"Bri, just because you think you're Magnum doesn't mean you get his luck. You certainly don't have his looks," Barbara teased.

"That's because he isn't as good-looking as *moi*." The man preened, earning boos and hisses from the group amid a shower of balled-up napkins.

"What do you propose to do?" Chad asked.

"Keep as close an eye on Caryn as possible," Sam said.

"I'm sure you'll volunteer for that hazardous duty," Brian brought up slyly. "Of course she won't be too happy about having a watchdog."

"After yesterday I don't think I'll get too much of an argument out of her," Sam said grimly, again feeling the fury he felt toward the attacker the first time he saw her injured face.

"So you're the one cleaning up Caryn's mess."

Sam wanted to wince as he looked across the room at Caryn's tight-lipped features. He'd noticed her and her mother's return a half hour ago and deliberately waited another hour before going over. Now he wasn't sure if it had been such a good idea. It hadn't taken him five minutes to figure out that Gerald Richards was one of the most chauvinistic men he had ever met and he treated his daughter more like some kind of dimwit than a highly intelligent woman.

"I wouldn't call it a mess, Mr. Richards," he spoke carefully, not wanting to insult the man no matter how much he didn't like him. "Sometimes these things happen. Unfortunately, Caryn was chosen to be the next victim."

Gerald turned toward his daughter. "If you had chosen to go into sports medicine you wouldn't have had all this happen to you."

"You're right, I wouldn't. Instead I could have been sued for malpractice or gotten tossed out on my ear because I pushed the team so hard some of the kids fell apart or had too many losing seasons," she said dryly, earning a cold glare from him.

"Your work must be very frustrating at times," Lisa cut in, smiling at Sam, her soft voice diffusing the situation.

Already liking the older woman, whom Caryn resembled so strongly, he had no trouble speaking warmly to her. "Yes, it does, but I just keep plugging away, and I have an excellent staff I can count on." Changing the subject, Sam said, "Are you planning on staying long?"

Lisa glanced at her husband. "Just a couple of days. Gerald's here to talk to a couple of high-school coaches. Then we're driving down to San Diego to see our son, Scott. He's a baseball coach at the university."

Sam nodded. He had never been fond of college sports, so thought it prudent not to say anything and further fan fires already burning hot.

"Caryn was an excellent runner in school. She won a great many awards," Gerald cut in, shooting a telling look at his daughter. "If she'd tried harder she could have had a go in the Olympics, but she didn't care to go the distance. Cameron, our oldest, was chosen for the team, but he was part of a senseless accident when another runner fell against him." His attitude intimated his feelings that the accident could have been deliberate. "That was when Cam got interested in sports medicine. He works in a clinic in Colorado. Very successful at it, too."

"I don't think what Caryn does is anything to sneeze at," Sam said mildly, fully aware he was entering a mine field, except now he couldn't have cared less, as long as the danger was directed at him. "I admit I'm not much when it comes to health and fitness, but I've seen a few issues, and what I've read has been very comprehensive. Her staff works hard to bring the message across in an informative way that doesn't preach. And we all know people tend to ignore anyone who's too pushy, so I think she's done a wonderful job in getting away from that." He smiled blandly at Gerald who sat there unsure if he had just been insulted. Caryn's head dipped down, her fingers covering her lips while Lisa looked away. "Well, I must be going." Sam stood up. "It was good to meet you, Mr. Richards, Mrs. Richards." His smile was warmer when bestowed on the older woman.

Gerald's eyes were narrowed as he watched Sam leave.

"I sure hope you're not sleeping with a loser like that," he growled at his daughter.

"Gerry!"

"Don't worry, Mom, I can take care of this." Caryn's smile held no humor in it. "You know, Dad, out of everything else you've said, that has to be the most crass. I ran in almost every event there was in high school and college, although my heart wasn't in it. Ever since I can remember you never told me how well I did, only how I could have done better. How I could have shaved a couple seconds off my time if I had only worked harder. I'm very happy with what I do, and I've gained a lot of respect in my field. I only wish you would see it that way." She was obviously gearing up for a big blowout.

"All right," Lisa cut in quietly. "Gerry, I think we should leave for Scott's today. You can meet with those coaches on our way back."

Caryn looked distressed. "Mom, I'm not trying to throw you out or anything."

She smiled. "I know that, but I also know the two of you. So I'll come down sometime on my own." Her eyes telegraphed a calming message to her daughter.

Caryn still felt guilty as she walked outside with her parents, standing by their car as her father loaded the suitcases into the trunk.

"We always seem to fight," she murmured, looking at her father as he slammed the lid down.

"I've only wanted the best for you," he told her in his harsh voice. "Is that so bad?"

She was determined to hold her ground. "Only when you don't listen to what I want."

Lisa's leave-taking was more emotional as she hugged Caryn goodbye.

"Now, call more often," she instructed. "And don't mind your father. He's been a football coach, which he thinks makes him the next thing to being God, so he forgets not everyone sees him that way."

Caryn stood in the parking lot and watched the car leave.

"I thought they were going to stay a few extra days." Sam had walked up behind her.

She'd never felt more depressed and more in need of comfort. She turned around and slid her arms around his waist. Surprised by her action, he could only put his arms around her and hold her tightly against him.

"Right about now a hug would be very nice," she choked out. "Just for once I'd like to know that a man sees me as more than some cold-blooded woman or a failed athlete."

Chapter Twelve

Caryn stared at the glass of wine Sam had poured for her. After the warm, comforting hug he had given her, he steered her toward his place. "I don't drink very often. Too much alcohol gives me a headache."

"I don't think one glass will hurt you." He stood over her with his drink in his hand. "Was it my imagination, or do you and your father not get along?"

She laughed, the sound catching in her throat. "Our not getting along is an understatement. I believe it began when I was born a girl and promptly spit up all over him, and went on from there."

Sam sat on the edge of the coffee table facing her and leaned forward resting his arms on his thighs. "He obviously feels you were Olympic material."

She shook her head. "He feels it, not me. I enjoyed the running. In fact I still do, but I didn't like the competing—the way some kids would do anything to run. My brothers saw it Dad's way, though. They believed in winning, not in just doing a good job, because Dad didn't want that. He just wanted to boast about his champion kids. He was always out there pushing us to win while Mom stayed in the background telling us that we also had to remember good sportsmanship." She sighed. "This is a terrible thing to say, but sometimes I wonder why she even married him. Oh, I know she loves him, and once she told me that love tends to overlook the imperfections. So I guess she's the calming influence in the marriage. She's great at keeping Dad and me from each other's throats when we're together for longer than an hour."

"He doesn't approve of your working for the magazine, does he?" he asked quietly. "Doesn't the fact your work has something to do with health and fitness make any kind of difference, or do you need to do something more active than push a pencil?"

She shook her head. "To him, running a magazine is sissy work. Even though I've gained recognition for my writing and my administrative work, he still refuses to acknowledge it as something instructive and informative."

"What about your idea of a physical-fitness regimen? Doesn't that tell him you haven't slowed down over the years? The kind of schedule you keep would kill a lesser person. I sure know it would kill me," he said wryly.

"Ah, but I'm not in serious training, so it doesn't count." Caryn sipped her wine. She suddenly jumped to her feet. "You know what? I'm in the mood for a large pizza with the works. What do you say? I know a great place not far from here that makes the kind of pizza a person would die for. My treat."

Sam stood up. "If you're willing to pay I'm more than willing to drive."

A little over an hour later a stunned Sam sat in a booth and watched Caryn demolish more than half the oversized pizza with little effort.

"Where do you put it?" he demanded.

Caryn used a napkin to wipe tomato sauce from her fingers and lips. "I didn't have any lunch."

"Well, you sure made up for it," he muttered, grabbing the last piece before Caryn could get to it. "I'll probably be up half the night guzzling Alka-Seltzer to counteract the heartburn. This stuff is lethal. It's a good thing I don't have an ulcer or I'd be a dead man before morning. I will admit that I'm surprised you know about such great pizza. I didn't think you were into junk food."

She leaned back, looking more relaxed than Sam ever remembered seeing her. "Pizza is an excellent source of protein and carbohydrates. What hurts a person is all the toppings. Besides a pig-out once in a while doesn't hurt. Although I do think you were rude not to offer me the last slice."

"I didn't want you to suffer the agony of stuffing yourself." He offered her a beatific smile.

"You're so kind."

"Lee once said something about a recent outdoor shoot that went wrong," Sam said. "Something about a model Jay went crazy over? Trouble was she was laughing so hard she never finished the story."

Caryn began laughing.

"Okay, obviously the story is a barrel of laughs. Care to enlighten me?" he pleaded.

"We had a shoot on exercise clothing we photographed at the Arboretum in Arcadia, and Jay decided he was in love with one of the models. She was pretty new to the business." She giggled. "I admit she was absolutely gorgeous, and no man in his right mind could ignore her. Jay tried to impress her during the shoot with his expertise with a camera. What he didn't count on was that some of the pictures were being shot

near flowers he was allergic to." Caryn choked. "If
you could have seen him. Within minutes his eyes were
swollen and his nose was bright red and running. He
was so upset that his macho image was ruined that he
almost cried."

"That's not so funny," Sam protested. "All he
wanted to do was impress her. Is that so wrong?"

"Don't worry about Jay. Remember Melissa at the
picnic?"

"The tall brunette with the incredible legs?" Sam
grimaced under Caryn's telling look. "What can I say?
I'm a leg man. Oh, I get it. You mean she's the
model?"

Caryn nodded. "While Jay was agonizing over
Melissa, she told us later that he looked like a lost little boy and her heart went out to him. Naturally we
never told him that. He's still convinced it was his
masculine charm."

"No wonder we men feel outnumbered at times,"
he mumbled, finishing the last of his wine.

After they left the pizza parlor Sam suggested a
walk. "Come on, you should walk off those last two
pieces you ate." He took hold of her hand and they
walked around the small shopping center, stopping to
look in the windows.

"We're still freezing our butts off and they're
showing summer clothes," Sam groused, looking at a
colorful display of shorts and tank tops in one store.

"I can remember going in a store last summer and
the first thing I saw were heavy wool sweaters and
winter coats," Caryn commented. "All it did was
make me feel even hotter. Of course, by the time I'm
ready to buy winter clothes they're having their big
sales and bringing out their summer lines."

Sam glanced at her profile. He wondered if he would ever get tired of just looking at her. Even with her swollen black-and-blue eye, she still looked beautiful. He was amazed how comfortable she was with her looks and her body.

"It would be very easy to fall in love with you," he said quietly and very seriously.

Caryn's head snapped up, and she looked at him with something akin to shock. She shook her head slowly. "Oh, Sam, don't do that. You're too nice a man to get tangled up with me. Not to mention you don't really know me."

"You eat junk food probably once every ten years, you're a workaholic, you exercise more in a day than I probably do in a year, you have a sense of humor that needs to surface more, and your idea of relaxing is a walking marathon through the swap meet," he said promptly. "You're beautiful, your figure is definitely great, you have good teeth, and basically you're a cheap date. I like that in a woman."

Caryn's eyes looked incredibly sad. "If only it was that easy. I'm the first to admit I'm a complex woman, and I don't think there's one person in this whole world who knows me as well as they think they do. As for any kind of relationship, I just can't have one."

"Can't, or won't?"

"Both. To be honest, I have no time to give to one," she said bluntly.

He was unperturbed by her candor. "Sure you do. You just have to learn how to rearrange your time to allow special people in. You know, the more I think about it the more I feel convinced I was sent here to loosen you up. It's a good thing I'm an expert at this. Lady, you need all the help you can get." He pulled gently on her hand. "Come on, your lips are turning the same lovely shade of blue as your face, and we can't have that happening."

Realizing the air had indeed grown colder during their stroll down the sidewalk, Caryn zipped up her heavy jacket and buried her hands in the deep pockets as they walked back to Sam's car. As soon as he had the engine running for a few minutes he turned on the heater, and warm air blasted out through the vents, chasing the chill from the air.

"It's nice to know you have normal eating habits," Sam told her as they drove back to the complex. "It gives me hope that my job of turning you into a laid-back person won't be as difficult as I thought it would be."

"You just like the idea that I paid for dinner," Caryn teased.

"Yeah, that was nice, too. I'm not so much a chauvinist that I'll get upset if a woman wants to pay the bill." He activated the garage-door opener and pulled inside as the door slowly slid upward. He shut off the engine and turned in his seat, laying one arm across the back, his fingers resting close to her shoulder. "Want to come in and finish your wine?"

She shook her head. "I better get home. I brought some paperwork home with me that I'd hoped to have finished before tomorrow. I'm going to have to do it tonight. I'm speaking at a women's-club breakfast tomorrow, so I can't put it off."

Sam held up his hand. "Let me guess. Your talk is about eating plenty of greens, getting eight hours' sleep every night and exercising a minimum of three times a week."

She laughed. "No, it's about today's career woman dealing with stress." Caryn impulsively leaned over and kissed him lightly on the lips. "Thanks for being my friend, Sam."

Not content with that, he pulled her toward him. "If you're going to say thank-you, do it properly," he said huskily, nuzzling her ear.

Her breath caught in her throat. "I thought I did."

"Only if I wasn't such a close friend," he murmured, finding her earlobe with his lips. He tugged on it gently, working his tongue around the hammered-gold stud earring she wore. "Do you know my dad once told me that it used to be only fallen women who had pierced ears?"

"Actually it's women who continually lose one earring that have their ears pierced," she corrected, tipping her head to one side for better access. "I once had a large collection of earrings without mates, until I broke down and had them pierced."

"Personally, I find pierced ears very sexy." His breath warmed the tiny lobe.

Caryn closed her eyes, allowing the warm sensation of Sam's mouth moving around her ear and along her jaw to wash over her. Pretty soon she didn't want to remain passive but to actively participate. She twisted around in the seat and looped her arms around his neck, nipping at the beard-rough skin of his chin. When his mouth moved down to hers, her lips parted automatically, craving his taste. His tongue slid in easily, searching out every corner and withdrawing slightly before savoring her again.

"You taste like mushrooms," he murmured.

Caryn's eyes were closed and she looked as if she had just been transported to another world. "That's

funny. You taste of pepperoni," she said throatily.
"Perhaps we should try this again and see if we can
come up with any new tastes."

"What a great idea." He wasted no time in captur-
ing her mouth fully while his hand slid upward from
her waist to the slight fullness of her breast. When his
palm flattened against her, he could feel the pebbly
hardness of her nipple pressing against his hand under the thick layers of clothing. He wanted nothing
more than to slide his hand under her sweater and find
out what her bare skin felt like.

While Caryn's senses concentrated on Sam's kissing technique, her body kept reminding her that
something was sticking her in the chest. "Sam," she
moaned into his mouth, nibbling on his lower lip while
trying to draw back from him a couple of inches.
"Sam, your gearshift."

"Hmm?" He was too busy concentrating on de-
vouring her.

Caryn grabbed hold of his shoulders and finally
pushed herself away from him. "Sam, your gearshift
is practically puncturing my chest."

He chuckled at the pained expression on her face.
"Funny, I never used to notice things like that, although I am beginning to realize that these bucket
seats aren't as comfortable as I remembered them."

"I think it comes with age." Caryn opened her door
and let herself out. She waited as Sam walked around
the front of the car and put his hand on the small of
her back. "This is the time when we decide we're too
old to be necking in the front seat of a car."

"We could continue it inside, unless you prefer
trying out the backseat. There's no gearshift there,"
he suggested.

She hesitated for a fraction of a second before slowly shaking her head. "Let's be honest with each other, Sam. If I go inside with you, we won't just stop at kissing and we know it. And I'm not sure I'm ready for that."

"I wouldn't push you into something you weren't ready for," he argued.

"I know, but that doesn't mean that I might not change my mind." She'd acknowledged her attraction for him, and Sam silently gloried in it.

"Okay." He draped an arm around her shoulders as if he was her greatest pal in the world. "Come on, I'll walk you to your front door and leave you with a mind-blowing kiss. That's the least you can let me do."

She laughed, relieved he hadn't grown angry with her change of heart after the way she had kissed him back only moments before. She remembered how others had in the past, although she couldn't remember ever kissing anyone the way she just had Sam. "Agreed."

And Sam did just that, after allowing Caryn to unlock her door. He also gravely offered to come in and make sure no one was hiding under her bed, but she assured him there was no need, because her platform bed had no room underneath for anyone to hide.

The moment Caryn was alone, her smile disappeared. Her lighthearted evening with Sam had gone a long way in relaxing her, but not enough as far as she was concerned. Part of her was tempted to run back to Sam's and allow their beginning relationship to mature. The other part knew she wouldn't.

SAM SAT SLUMPED on the couch, a can of beer cradled between his hands. He was busy trying to figure out Caryn's relationship with her father, and all thoughts were depressing. She hadn't talked about the man before, and after meeting him he understood why.

"Why can't he be proud of her?" he spoke out loud. "What's so wrong with his acknowledging her accomplishments? No wonder she's trying to kill herself with work. She figures the more she does the better chance she has that he'll praise her. The sad thing is, I don't think he ever will." Draining the last of his beer, he slowly got up and carried the can into the kitchen, tossing it into the trash. Looking out, he should see lights burning from Caryn's windows. He took five seconds to think about it before he headed for his phone, picked up the receiver and dialed her number.

"Yes?"

"Do you always answer the phone that way? Some guys could get the wrong idea." He cradled the receiver between his chin and shoulder.

Caryn laughed softly. "Such as you."

"Yeah, for one." Sam paused. "I know it's pretty late to be calling, but there was something I wanted you to know." He went on before he lost his nerve. "It's more than obvious that your dad has always been an overachiever and expected his kids to be the same way." He could feel the tension rolling across the wires at the mention of her father. "You see, my dad was the exact opposite. He was so laid back he could fall asleep in the middle of a sentence, and no, he didn't suffer from sleeping sickness. He was just relaxed all the time. So as a result my brother and I had to be first in everything. Since he was five years older than me I felt I had to beat all his records or go out and make new ones of my own. A couple of times I did both. I was on the debating team because I have that great gift of gab, and my brother went out for sports. He even went to college on a football scholarship. Mark got his degree, went on for a master's and went to work for a Wall Street firm. In no time he was making money hand over fist, didn't know, or care, what a vacation was and had no time for anyone, even his family." His voice drifted off for a moment, then came back as strong as ever. "I was seriously thinking about law school when I got out of the service. Then my parents got word that Mark had a stroke. I was able to get emergency leave, and we flew back East and arrived there just in time to see him. The doctor said that he had basically worked himself to death. Mark didn't bother taking any time to relax and recharge his batteries. He was also a heavy smoker and drinker, and the added stress from his work didn't help, but he had been warned many times." Sam paused for a moment. "The trouble was he didn't listen. My dad was a broken man after that, because he was afraid it was somehow his fault."

"Why?" she asked in a hushed voice that sounded as if she was on the verge of tears. "Your brother lived his life the way he wanted to. Your father couldn't have done anything to stop him."

"No, but he knew we turned out the way we did because for some crazy reason we didn't want to be like him," he said quietly. "After some lengthy soul-searching I decided an early death wasn't worth it. So now I take the time to stop and smell the flowers and I haven't regretted it since. Caryn, Mark was only twenty-seven when he died. He didn't like Dad's way of life, so he made his own and it killed him. I decided I didn't want to end up like my brother, so I changed my life. You didn't like the way your father ran your life, so you made you own, although it isn't all that different. He made football his life. You have the magazine. And stress can kill just as easily as heart disease or a bullet. I don't want that to happen to you. I care for you too much, so I would appreciate it if you would think over what I've said." Without saying another word he carefully hung up the receiver, steeling himself against the soft sound of her crying on the other end. Feeling incredibly weary, Sam returned to the living room and slumped on the couch. He tipped his head back and looked up.

"I'm not going to let her do it, Mark," he said grimly. "She still has a choice. I just hope she makes the right one."

CARYN SAT at her drawing board making no move to work. She had come up to the loft after Sam's phone call. She'd had no idea his past carried such darkness. It explained why he tried so hard to urge her to slow down and find a world other than her work.

"And he's always been there to show me," she murmured, staring down into her box of pastel chalks before selecting a color. "Well, perhaps I could begin to show him a little something of me." With that said, she lost herself in her work and forgot all sense of time.

Caryn knew exactly what she wanted to do, and before long the picture was taking shape. Usually it took a while for a picture to form itself in her mind, but not this time. Being the perfectionist she was, she usually reworked an idea several times. Not this time. Before long the picture of two young boys playing in a flower-strewn field with an older man looking on in the background formed. The pastels gave it a dreamlike haze, which was exactly what she wanted. She lost track of the hours passing. All that mattered was the scene in front of her.

Chapter Thirteen

"I come bearing gifts," Caryn said shyly, her cheeks tinted with a hint of pink.

Sam stood back, unsure whether to feel surprised by her impromptu visit or the fact that she appeared to be blushing. He decided to remain quiet about both, for fear she'd get mad and walk away.

"I've never been known to turn down a gift." He looked curiously at the large wrapped package Caryn carried. "Should I confess now that it isn't my birthday and Christmas is long gone?" He led the way into the living room. "Would you like something to drink? I even have some diet Coke floating around."

"That sounds wonderful." She acted as if she was grabbing onto the offer as it were a lifeline. She looked around the room with its sofa of rust-brown and cream, and a rust-colored easy chair adjacent to it. "I should have told you before I like what you've done with the room. I'm impressed. These colors go very well with the carpet."

"I was surprised that I could find something that matched," he said with a chuckle as he walked toward the kitchen.

"So what have you been doing the past few days?" he called out.

"Getting the latest issue of the magazine ready. We all stayed late a couple of nights because two articles ended up running a bit long and they needed cutting, and all sorts of last-minute horrors that seem to happen just before a deadline." She looked around the room, noticing the lack of personal touches, and mentally placed a vase of dried flowers on a table near the patio door. She noticed something sitting on the stereo set near the stairs and walked over to study it.

"It's an air filter," Sam explained, walking back into the room. "Just because I smoke doesn't mean I like the room to smell that way, and during the winter it's too cold to air it out."

"Good idea," she agreed, accepting the glass and drinking deeply. "Thanks. It's been a long and dry day."

Sam frowned, seeing the faint lines of weariness bracketing her face. "Did you eat any dinner?"

"Yes."

"Why do I hear a fib in that word?"

She smiled. "Because you want to." She looked down at the package resting on the carpet against her knees. "I guess I should get this over with and let you open it." She picked it up and held it out. "I hope you like it."

Sam read more into those five words than perhaps Caryn meant to be heard. He accepted the package with reverence.

"I can't remember the last time I got a gift for no reason," he murmured. "On second thought, I can. I'm sure this won't be the same."

"What kind of gift could that be?" Caryn asked curiously.

He flushed. "Trust me. Not for little girls' ears."

"But a woman gave it to you," she pressed.

"She gave me a pair of underwear made out of two rubber bands. I got rid of them after my mother found them. Are you happy now?" Sam ripped away the paper and soon realized he was holding a metal-framed picture. He turned it around and stared long and hard at the picture done in soft pastels. "Oh, Caryn." His voice was hushed. "I...ah, I don't know what to say. It's beautiful."

She sat there still looking unsure. Sam looked down at her. "This is some of your work, isn't it?" he asked softly, waiting until she nodded. "Caryn, do you honestly realize how talented you are?"

She laughed, suddenly acting as if it was nothing special. "It's just something I do."

"Don't act so blasé about something this beautiful," he chided. "Hey, I can't draw a straight line with the help of a ruler." He held the picture out, studying the two little boys and the man standing in the background. "This is supposed to be me and my brother with my father, isn't it?"

Caryn nodded. "That night after you called on the phone I sat down at my drawing table and it suddenly came to me. I ended up working on it almost all night because it refused to leave my head. I couldn't bring it over sooner since I had this issue to wrap up and I wanted to find a frame for the picture."

Sam immediately went into the kitchen and came out holding a hammer and nail. Within moments the picture was hanging on the wall facing them. He stood back, adjusting the frame until he felt it was even.

"Perfect," he announced.

"I just hope Dave doesn't mind your putting holes in his wall," she said dryly, but pleased that he thought so highly of it.

Sam walked over to her with a wicked gleam in his eye. "And now to thank the artist," he murmured, taking her glass out of her hand and setting it on the coffee table. He grasped her forearms and slowly pulled her to her feet.

Caryn chewed her lower lip as she looked up at him. "Just your putting it up is more than enough thanks."

"Oh no, that isn't nearly enough in my book." His head lowered until his mouth rested just above hers. "I used to think a woman over five foot three was too tall. Since then I've discovered that taller women have a very nice advantage."

"Oh, such as?" Her breath warmed him.

"Such as I don't have to bend down as far to kiss you." His lips moved gently over hers for a brief second. "I'm still not sure I like the idea of looking you practically in the eye when we talk, but I can live with it."

Caryn's hands moved restively on his waist, her fingers digging into his skin just above his jeans waistband. She tipped her head back a fraction. "Sam, are you trying to seduce me?" she asked in a husky voice.

He looked hopeful. "Am I succeeding?"

"I think so." Sam's smile was slow and incredibly sexy in Caryn's eyes. "I should leave." She was well aware she didn't sound convincing.

"I still haven't thanked you for the picture."

"Yes, you did."

"Not the way I wanted to." Sam inhaled the soft fragrance of Caryn's perfume and knew he would never smell the scent again without thinking of her. He pulled her closer to him until her breast grazed his chest. "It's been building up to this for a long time, Caryn, and I think you know it, too."

She swallowed what felt like a rock in her throat. "Sam, I don't sleep around."

He smiled, recognizing her hesitation and adoring her all the more. "Neither do I, although I do have to confess that I'm not a virgin. Does that alter your feelings toward me?"

Caryn bit her lip to keep from laughing. "Oh, Sam, how do you do it?"

"Like this." His time of teasing was over as he kissed her thoroughly, his tongue a welcome invasion in her mouth. He wrapped his arms around her, holding her warmly in his embrace as he proceeded to kiss every inch of her face. "You smell so sexy," he said hoarsely, his lips feathering her eyelashes. "The first time I met you and smelled that perfume that makes me think of spring, I thought you were the most gorgeous woman I had ever met."

Her laugh almost sounded like a faint moan. "Come off it, Sam. You thought I was a hard-nosed broad out to give you a bad time."

"That, too. But I still thought you were gorgeous." He breathed heavily as his hands moved up and down her back, massaging the last bit of resistance from her body. "Oh, Caryn, do you know how good you feel against me? How good you taste?"

"As good as you are to me?" she whispered, drawing back just enough so that he could edge his hands under the hem of her sweater and trace a searing path along her skin. When he touched her breasts she held back a moan of pleasure, but her swiftly drawn breath was easily heard.

"Caryn, if I take off your sweater you won't hit me or anything, will you?"

Her answer was to step back and pull the garment off over her head. All she wore was a sheer bra in a pale peach that seemed to glow against her skin.

It was then Sam realized Caryn appeared a bit unsure of his reaction. He couldn't believe she might be uneasy about her body, and he made sure she had nothing to worry about.

"You are so beautiful," he breathed, half wanting to pull her back into his arms and half wanting to carry her upstairs to his bed but afraid she might object. "Caryn, do you realize how much I want to make love to you?"

Her face lit up as if he had said the magic words. "As much as I want to make love to you?"

Sam threw back his head and laughed deeply. "Now that's the kind of good news I like to hear." Without further ado he picked her up.

"Sam, I'm too heavy for you!" she protested, laughing as he walked toward the stairs.

"Are you kidding?" He carried her upstairs, then down the hallway, placing her on a water bed, which undulated gently under her. "See?" He pulled his shirt out of his jeans and began unbuttoning it until Caryn sat up and swatted his hands away, releasing each button with great care and bestowing a kiss on his chest each time more hair-roughened skin was revealed.

"You're breathing hard," she whispered, against the slightly damp skin.

"Actually I think that has something to do with what you're doing to me," he rasped, allowing his shirt to drop behind him. He combed his fingers through her heavy mass of hair, watching it curl around his hands.

She blew into his navel. "Do you want me to stop?"

"No way!" But soon Sam had other ideas. He knelt on the bed beside Caryn and leaned over to unfasten her jeans. He swore under his breath when the zipper proved more than a little difficult to unfasten. When her jeans finally lay in a heap at the foot of the bed he was able to feast his eyes on the rest of her body. The tiny triangle she wore was the same color as her bra. "You really know how to drive a guy crazy, don't you?" He stretched out next to her and brought her back into his arms. Caryn draped one leg over his as their lips met hungrily, words of love said in raspy voices as they sipped and nibbled on one another's skin.

"With you I feel positively decadent," she murmured throatily, fastening her teeth on his earlobe and pulling on it. "Um, I want to be all the woman you'll ever need." She could feel the golden haze surround her as she lost herself in her senses while running her hands over his chest and feeling the heat emanate from his body. "Perhaps I should tell you I'm not usually this forward."

"Then I'm glad you're this way with me." Sam unfastened her bra and carefully drew the edges back. He smiled at the pouting dusky-pink nipples and lowered his head to nibble one. Caryn moaned and wrapped her hands around his head pulling him down to her. He curled his tongue around the pebbled surface, listening to her soft words of love while he feasted on her satiny skin. "I could keep telling you how beautiful you are, but I don't want to repeat myself."

Caryn smiled as she kissed the top of his head, enjoying the feel of his hair against her lips. "That's all right. Keep telling me," she murmured. "But first, don't you think you're a little overdressed?" One of her hands wandered down to his belt buckle and slowly released it. The snap was quickly taken care of and the zipper lowered just as easily. "Do you think you could manage to take these off?"

Sam levered upward and almost tore his jeans off, throwing them across the room where they landed in a heap by the door. His briefs were tossed in the opposite direction along with Caryn's bra. When he carefully inched off her underwear, he pressed a kiss in the middle of her abdomen.

"As much as I hate to be practical at a time like this, are you protected?" he murmured, crawling back toward her.

"Yes." She welcomed him back into her arms and showered his face with kisses that began with his mouth and ended in a lengthy trail across his chest. She pushed him onto his back and leaned over him, exploring with her hands as she found his nipples peeking saucily out of a mat of golden brown hair. Wanting to give him pleasure, she touched the tip of her tongue to one brown nub and laughed softly when Sam almost shot off the bed.

They took their time, fighting the urgency roaring in their veins as they explored one another's bodies with great care. Caryn found Sam's appendectomy scar and proceeded to kiss it better. Sam discovered an intriguing birthmark on Caryn's hip and enjoyed tracing it first with his fingertip then with his lips.

When the time came for them to become one they knew it was more than right. They looked deep into one another's eyes as Sam slowly merged his body with hers, stopping to allow her to be comfortable with him as he realized she hadn't had a lover for a while.

"It never felt like this before," Caryn whispered, looking up at him with eyes that shone like burning amber.

He smiled, silently agreeing with her. "Why are you whispering?"

"Because something this special should be handled with awe. And I want you to know how wonderful you are." She flexed her hips a tiny bit, and left Sam groaning through his soft laughter.

They moved together as if they had been lovers for years. Sam kept murmuring that Caryn was made so perfectly. He wanted to believe she was made just for him. Their movements were synchronized as they flew faster and farther into the sun, before Sam felt the explosion rock his body with Caryn following him, a soft cry on her lips.

They had no idea how long they lay locked together in a tumble of damp limbs regaining their breath. Sam lay on his side, his arms around Caryn while he used his fingers to comb her hair away from her face.

"Whatever I dreamed of before was nothing compared to the real thing," he murmured, dropping a kiss on her ear.

She knew she was probably smiling idiotically, but she didn't care. "I didn't dare dream."

He shifted a bit, nuzzling her skin and tasting the salty texture. "Why not?" He felt tension invade her body. "Why, Caryn?" he pressed.

She sighed. "I was engaged a few years ago. It didn't work out."

"You two fell out of love? Better to happen before the wedding than after." He didn't want to admit the relief he felt that she hadn't gone through with it, even though he could sense it had hurt her a great deal. He just hoped she still didn't hold any feelings toward the man, then reminded himself she couldn't have made such passionate love with him if that were so.

Caryn hesitated. "I guess you could say that. I guess you'd say I wasn't the person he thought I was." She turned onto her side and began kissing him feverishly. "I don't want to think about him now. Not when I'm with you." She began seducing Sam with her lips and hands until he couldn't do anything but make love to her again with the same explosive results. After that they remained close together as they fell into an exhausted sleep.

Caryn woke barely an hour later feeling a depression fall over her like a dark cloud of sadness. She looked at Sam, who still slept peacefully, his hair tousled, making him look more a boy than the man she knew he was. She carefully edged her way out of bed and groped for his shirt, slipping it on before creeping out of the room. Downstairs, she didn't feel the peace she did at home, even as she stared into the darkness at the pastel artwork on the wall. She sat curled up on the couch unable to push away the fear that the day would come when Sam would look at her with the same disgust Alex had. The more she thought about it the greater her pain, and the tears slid down her cheeks. Caryn buried her face in her hands, feeling the pain wash over her like a heavy mantle.

Sam lay upstairs hearing the muted sounds of Caryn's crying and closed his eyes. He didn't know how he sensed her tears had nothing to do with their lovemaking, but it had triggered something. He wondered if it didn't have something to do with her former fiancé. He ached to go downstairs and take her into his arms and assure her nothing would ever hurt her again, but he knew if he did she would only withdraw, and he couldn't bear that happening.

"Your barrier is coming down, Caryn, my love," he whispered into the darkness, "and it appears with it comes the hurt. But don't worry, just as long as I'm around the hurt will go away. That I promise you."

"I'M NOT THE GREATEST COOK in the world, so scrambled eggs are your best bet," Sam told Caryn. "They're my greatest achievement, because I tend to break the yolks when I crack the shells."

"Just coffee is fine." She ducked her head, her hair hiding her face from him.

Sam immediately leaned across the table, taking two fingers to lift her chin. "No more hiding, Caryn," he said gently. "We shared something incredible last night, and this morning wasn't too bad either. I don't want you feeling ashamed."

"I don't. I guess I'm just not sure how to treat the 'morning after,'" she confessed.

"We're both doing just fine. I was the gentleman and allowed you to have the shower first and didn't even try to attack you in it." He appeared proud of himself. "Believe me, it took a lot of willpower."

A smile tipped the corners of her lips upward. "No, it didn't. I locked the bathroom door."

"That, too." Sam poured them each another cup of coffee. "Hey, call in sick today."

"What?"

"Call in sick. You know, tell them you have typhoid or the black plague or something," he suggested his eyes alight. "We'll play hooky. What do you say?"

"I don't know." Caryn shook her head, sorely tempted to give in to his whimsical idea. "I've never done it."

He reared back his head in shock. "Never done it? Well, we're just going to have to remedy that right now." He got up and walked over to the phone and brought the receiver to her. "I would have dialed Pat's number but I don't know it."

Caryn put in the call before she lost her nerve. "Pat? Hi, it's me. Oh, it's that early?" She shot Sam a dark look. "I'm sorry, I guess I didn't look at the time. I'm not feeling up to par today, so I think I'll remain home in bed." She rolled her eyes as her secretary obviously delivered a lecture. "No, it isn't because of all the overtime I've been putting in. I have a sore throat and my head feels a bit stuffed, so I hope to stop this cold before it escalates into something nasty." She pushed Sam's wandering hand away from her and shook her finger at him. "Yes, I'll stay in bed and drink plenty of orange juice. In fact, I'm going to try to sleep this off, so I'll just leave the answering machine on. Okay, thanks." She tossed him the receiver and watched him deftly replace it. "That was dirty pool, Russell. I'm sure Pat was suspicious. I'm never sick!"

"I did like that part about staying in bed all day." He picked the receiver up and tossed it from one hand to the other before quickly punching out a number. "Hi, yeah, I know what time it is. I'm not coming in to the office today. I want to run some leads down, and any calls that need to be made can be done from here, so you can play boss for the day. Good." With that he hung up. "See how easy that was?"

"Except your lie was bigger that mine. Run down some leads?" She looked at him with disbelief. "Give me a break."

He flashed her a broad grin. "Wrong, that's exactly what I'm going to do, and I'm going to let you tag along. So head across the way and hurry into unwrinkled clothes. We've got a long drive ahead of us."

No matter how hard Caryn tried to pry the destination out of Sam, he merely smiled and shook his head as they drove onto the freeway a half hour later heading north.

"Just sit back and enjoy the ride," he advised. "This is one of those times when I regret having bucket seats, otherwise you could have slid over here next to me and made the trip more enjoyable."

"Just as well. You really should keep both hands on the wheel." She plucked his hand off her knee and plopped it back on the steering wheel.

Forty minutes later Caryn looked at the expanse of ocean on her left. "Obviously we're taking the coastal route, and since we don't have enough time to drive to San Francisco for lunch it must be some place closer."

"You could say that," Sam said with a mysterious air.

They stopped in one of the tiny seaside towns and picked up drinks and some snacks to eat in the car, while Sam promised Caryn a special lunch when they reached their destination.

"I think Jenkins is the man we're looking for," he told her as they drove up the Pacific Coast Highway.

"You told me he's on one of those extended cruises," she replied.

"That's what his secretary says and for all we know she believes it. I don't, so I asked Lieutenant Kendall to do some checking. It appears Jenkins applied for a business license in Santa Barbara under his wife's name. Guess what kind of business?"

"Something to do with fitness?"

Sam beamed. "You got it. Now, if his wife is working to get a new business off the ground, why would he be out of state instead of staying home helping her with the day-to-day hassles? Not to mention overseeing his new company, which sells fitness equipment on television. One thing he doesn't do is give up."

"Could he be trying to get more working capital?"

He shook his head. "No, there's more to it than that. I'm sure of it. All I want to do is take a look around and see if I can notice anything unusual. We've checked out his L.A. offices and haven't gotten anywhere there."

"Then you don't want me with you, because he knows what I look like," she pointed out.

"I don't intend either one of us to be seen," he assured her. "We'll be there soon, and if I think anything looks out of line I'll stash you somewhere and come back for you later."

"Give me a break, Sam. We're not part of a Humphrey Bogart detective movie," Caryn informed him.

When they reached the outskirts of a well-known coastal town, Sam again checked his map and a piece of paper he had resting on the dashboard. He drove through an older part of town and checked the small companies there that boasted custom-made bikinis in one building and surfboards in the next. At the end of one street he found what he was looking for. He drove around the corner and parked where they couldn't be seen.

"Dance wear," Caryn breathed. "It would make sense. There's also a sign that advertises aerobic shoes and clothing. What next?"

"We'll just sit tight and see if anything happens." He leaned back and took her hand between his two. "It's almost lunchtime, so someone should be leaving soon. I especially would like to see who's driving that new Mercedes parked along the side."

It was a half hour before their question was answered. A tall, heavyset man walked out a side door and headed straight for the shiny white car.

"Well?" Sam asked, not bothering to turn his head.

"He's heavier, the gray in his hair is gone, but it's still Jenkins," Caryn said, confirming his hunch. "Now what?"

"We have lunch and I tell Kendall." Sam waited to see where the Mercedes would go and then waited another fifteen minutes before starting up his engine. "If you see a white Mercedes, scrunch down in the seat. We don't want to tip him off yet. Okay?"

She nodded. "Then we don't dare stay in town."

"We won't, although I'd like to come up here for a long weekend sometime." He looked around the Spanish-style town with interest. "Think you'd be interested?"

Caryn looked at him with a warm and promising smile. "I guess I could make an exception for you."

Sam headed inland and they were soon driving on Route 154, a more scenic way that passed Lake Cachuma. Caryn noticed several trucks and campers parked in the camping facilities.

"Considering the route you're taking I'd hazard a guess you're heading for Solvang," she commented.

"The lady is so clever. I'm in the mood for some good old-fashioned Danish cooking, and since we're so close I decided to indulge that craving. I figured you wouldn't mind. At least, I hope not." He sighed. "Brian said it's a great place."

"No, I don't mind at all. In fact I'm going to enjoy watching your reaction to a town that has several restaurants, bakeries, not to mention fudge kitchens, on practically every street. Oh yes, Solvang is definitely your kind of town."

Sam groaned with delight. "Now I know I'm in heaven. Don't worry, honey. You're not left out of that thought."

Chapter Fourteen

"I feel as if I've been transported to another country." Sam looked around the copper-roofed buildings, windmills and wooden storks. Because of the cold day and the fact that tourist season wasn't in full force yet, he'd had no problem finding a parking space in one of the public lots. They had opted to walk through the town. They stopped at one hotel that looked as if it had come out of a fairy tale. He turned to Caryn, who stood beside him hanging on to his hand. "You could always say your cold hasn't gotten any better and I could say I'm still on the road," he suggested huskily. "I'd even spring for a toothbrush."

Caryn hesitated, surprised at herself for even thinking of doing something impulsive. "Sam, we can't do this now. Not with all that's going on. I wish we could."

He lifted his face to the sky and shouted, "Hallelujah, the woman does care if she's willing to put me before her job!"

Her faced burned a bright red. "Sam!" She hastily put her hand over his mouth. When she tried to remove it he grasped her wrist and pressed his mouth against the center of her palm, the tip of his tongue darting out to finish his kiss. His eyes danced with devilish delight as he watched her reaction. "People are watching us," she whispered, finally able to retrieve her hand.

"They're happy to see two people in love." He captured her hand and kept it close to his side as they walked along.

Caryn felt the pit of her stomach drop at least a mile. "Sam."

He held up his other hand to indicate silence. "I know. You don't want to admit the truth, but—" he stopped and spun her around to face him "—you have no choice. You took advantage of me last night, Caryn. I don't want you to lose your respect for me because of what happened."

Strangled sounds left her throat. "You are a very sick man."

He leaned forward and whispered in her ear. "Yes, I am. I'm sick for you."

Caryn stepped around him and walked swiftly down the sidewalk, but Sam wasn't about to let her get away.

"Hey, don't worry. I don't expect any declarations right away," he confided, linking his fingers through hers. "Just as long as you can squeeze me in between everything else I'll be happy." He suddenly skidded to a stop. "Oh, I have to try some of these." He reached for his wallet and paid for a paper plateful of *aebleskivers*, Danish pancakes.

"They're best with raspberry jam," the clerk told him.

His eyes lit up. "Do you have any?"

They found a bench while Sam dipped the round pancakes, dusted with powdered sugar, into the jam and bit into the first one. He shared the second one with Caryn. He ignored her protests that she didn't want any jam with it and held the tempting morsel to her lips.

"This is not a town to be in when you're on a diet," Caryn decided, watching Sam finish the last pancake. "Where on earth do you put all this food?"

He shrugged. "As I said before, my family just doesn't gain weight. When I was in high school my mother had me drink special shakes so I wouldn't look too scrawny."

She groaned, "And if I look at something the wrong way I gain weight."

Sam looked at her closely. "Is that why you exercise so much and watch everything you eat? Because you gain weight easily?"

She looked down at the ground, uneasy with bringing up another piece of her inner self that she would have preferred kept hidden. "Exercise helps burn calories," was all she said.

Sam opened his mouth, prepared to ask more about it but decided this wasn't the time to push the issue.

"Come on, let's walk off the food." He stood up and pulled her to her feet. "Look at all the shops you can drag me into."

"Careful, I might take you up on it," she warned playfully.

Pretty soon Caryn couldn't resist the many intriguing shops and took Sam at his word. At the first one that specialized in handmade candles she wandered from one display to the other. Unable to resist, she bought a large pale blue candle that had multishaded curlicues along the sides. At the next store she decided to explore she went from one hand-carved brightly painted nutcracker to another.

"I wonder how many pounds that is," Sam mused, watching two people pour a large vat of just-cooked fudge onto a huge marble slab, where they worked with the dark chocolate mass, smoothing it into one-pound slabs.

"Ugh! Just looking at it is enough to send me into sugar shock." Caryn grimaced.

"I want to buy some." Sam pulled her inside. "Maybe even take some back in to the office."

"You won't be able to take any into the office or they'll know you were playing hooky," she pointed out with a smug smile.

"I was in Santa Barbara working on the case," he countered, staring at the many flavors. "This is just a side trip. Hmm, this could be tough."

"Why not just buy one, because you might find something else at another shop," Caryn suggested.

"Good idea." A few minutes later they left, Sam carrying a box of rich chocolate fudge with walnuts.

They wandered inside a few of the many shops and came out with something. Pretty soon Sam purchased a large shopping bag to hold everything.

"I can't believe what we've bought," Caryn laughed, looking through their varied purchases. They had taken time to sit on a bench and warm themselves with cups of coffee. "Let's see, a hand-knitted shawl for your mother, a nutcracker for my sister-in-law's birthday, an *aebleskiver* pan for your father—I still can't believe he does the cooking in your family—amaretto, coconut-mint and rum fudge, that cute little dress for your niece, a special blend of coffee, herb teas for me, pipe tobacco for I don't remember who..." She looked up at him. "Don't you think you overdid it just a bit with the fudge?"

"Look who's talking? You were the one who bought five pounds for your cleaning lady."

She wrinkled her nose. "I know. Bad move, but she loves chocolate, and she'll be stunned that I bought some for her. What next?"

Sam consulted his watch. "How about some dinner? By the time we finish eating the traffic going home shouldn't be too bad."

"I'm sure I won't be able to talk you out of it."

They soon learned their choice of restaurants was varied. They chose a tiny one near the outskirts of town where they ate open-face sandwiches popular in Denmark.

"Their beer looked inviting, but not with me driving," Sam commented as they walked back to their car.

As they drove away Caryn turned in her seat, looking back at what she considered was one of the most fun days in her life.

"It's so peaceful there," she mused, curling her legs under her. "It's so much the opposite of L.A., which I guess is why I appreciate the quiet. Yet I'm sure if I lived here I'd go crazy within days."

"You might not. Maybe a place like this is exactly what you need," Sam countered. "After all, how long have you been with the magazine? Five, six years?"

"Six and a half." She shifted her position, unsure if she liked the direction of their conversation.

"And how long since your last vacation?"

Now she knew she didn't like this line of talk. "I don't know."

Undaunted by her terse reply, he continued pressing. "Last year? The year before?"

"I said I don't know!"

Without looking at her, Sam reached for Caryn's hand and brought it over to rest on his thigh with his hand covering it. "I was right. I got here just in time," he murmured.

"I'm getting tired of your supposition that you're rescuing a lost cause or something," she said crossly.

Sam brought her hand to his lips and kissed the skin between her thumb and forefinger. "Can the chatter, kiddo. I know you too well now."

Caryn turned to him, staring into his eyes with an enigmatic smile on her face. "Do you?"

Not wanting to talk any longer, Caryn rested her head back and closed her eyes. Pretty soon she was asleep. Sam looked over, noticing her even breathing. The more time he spent with her, the greedier he grew for her company, but he felt frustrated that he had to caution himself to take it easy, for fear of scaring her. Sometimes he thought it was only pure luck she hadn't backed away from him.

"Nope, it's my masculine charm," he reminded himself under his breath, now wanting to get home as soon as possible with the hope he could persuade her to spend the night with him again.

"No, Sam," she refused gently as they stood by her front door. "We both have to go to work tomorrow, and knowing you, we wouldn't get more than twenty minutes' sleep tonight."

"You really think we'd get that much?"

"Sam." She shook her head, laughing. She sobered and covered his cheek with her hand. "We're still moving a bit fast and I need to get a few things straight in my head, okay?''

He sighed. "Okay, but that doesn't mean I like it."

"I'm sure you don't."

Sam wrapped his arms around her and took his time kissing her. "I didn't think you'd argue with a good-night kiss," he whispered, when they finally came up for air.

Caryn leaned limply against him. "I don't think I had a choice. Where did you learn to be such a good kisser, anyway? Or do I not want to know about that?"

"Marcy Anne Wilson in the ninth grade," he said promptly. "Let me tell you she was a redheaded, hot-blooded kisser. She really knew how to keep the fires burning, and I was a more than willing learner. Of course, you realize I was very advanced for my age."

"In the ninth grade I concentrated on running relay races. Obviously I missed out on something." Caryn moved out of his arms and inserted her key in the lock. "Good night, Sam."

He brought her back for another quick hard kiss. "Don't worry, I'll behave. But could you think about meeting for lunch at some out-of-the-way place where I could nibble on your ear without worrying about running into anyone at work?"

"After playing hooky I have no idea what I'll be walking into. Why don't you call me in the morning and I'll see what things look like."

Content with that, Sam handed Caryn her purchase and walked away, watching until she was inside and he heard the bolt on the door.

Caryn pulled off her jacket and hung it in the closet. After leaving her packages on the kitchen table she walked upstairs, stopping by the phone set near her drawing board when she saw the red light blinking on the answering machine. A part of her suggested she check her messages tomorrow when she didn't feel so tired. The other part ordered her to do it now. Sighing, she pressed the bar that rewound the tape.

"Hi, Caryn." Pat's voice sounded hurried. "Caryn, you around?" Silence for a few seconds. "Okay, when you wake up would you give me a call at home? The fire sprinklers went off and the offices are a mess. Sorry to ruin your free day. In fact I would be happier if you were off somewhere with Sam than staying home in bed with a cold. I tried calling him but he's out of the office today, so Brian came down. Take care and don't forget your vitamin C."

Caryn watched the tape rewind with weary resignation. "The one day I take off and this happens," she murmured. "Why is someone trying to take control away from me?" Feeling the familiar tension hit her body, she went into the bathroom for a long hot shower and slipped on her robe. Knowing there would be no sleep for her that night, she returned downstairs. She intended to keep her control any way she could.

"HOW DID IT HAPPEN?" Sam demanded, hearing the news the moment he entered his office.

Brian shook his head. "Building Maintenance said it was a malfunction. I don't buy it. I'm sorry you had to get hit with it the minute you got in, Sam, but you didn't call in yesterday, and I guess your answering machine at home was off."

Sam sighed, raking his fingers through his hair as he wished he could find the right answers. "Yeah, I guess

I lost track of time when I was up in Santa Barbara checking out Jenkins. I called Lieutenant Kendall early this morning, and he's promised to do some checking on him for me. I feel it in my gut that Jenkins is the one behind this. How much damage to the magazine's offices?"

"Carpets are soaked, papers on top of the desks were ruined. That type of thing. They had a crew in there all night with those heavy-duty vacuums that suck up water," Brian replied. "Caryn was home sick," Sam felt a twinge when her name was mentioned. "Pat tried calling her but only got her answering machine."

Sam turned away. Had Caryn checked her machine last night? No, she couldn't have, because if she'd heard that kind of news wouldn't she have called him? Yet, would she have honestly passed by her machine if the message light was blinking? He didn't want to think about the answer.

"You know you've got some angry women out there," Brian kidded, bringing Sam back to the present.

"What?"

He grinned. "All that fudge you brought in. They're all on diets."

"They don't have to eat it."

"Sure, tell them that. It will probably be gone by lunchtime." Brian gave him a quizzical look. "Sam, you okay? You seem to be off in another world."

Sam recovered quickly. "It's this problem with the magazine. I feel as if someone is playing games with us, and I can't see the end."

Brian hesitated. "Then you're going to be even angrier when you see this." He handed him a newspaper, one of the pages folded back.

Sam's temper rose the moment he read the headline. "So the reporter thinks mismanagement is causing some of the problems," he gritted, tossing the paper on his desk. "How the hell did she find out about all of this? I thought we had kept this pretty well under wraps."

"Barbara's over there now trying to find out the woman's source."

"Caryn's going to go through the roof if she reads this."

"I called Pat, and she told me Caryn doesn't take this paper. She's advised we hold off for a little while before telling her about the article. At least until we hear from Barbara and see what she's learned."

Sam nodded. "Okay. Now, you're traveling up to Portland, right?"

"Yeah, I'm on this afternoon's flight. I just wanted to come in to show you the paper."

The two men shook hands.

"Good luck up there," Sam told him.

"Hey, if anyone needs the luck, it's you, old buddy. See you next Monday. If you need any kind of support you know where I am."

Sam glanced at the offending newspaper and cursed softly. "Buck up, Caryn, we're on the last lap. I feel it. I just hope you won't back out when all this is over."

"Mr. Gregory, I had no idea someone would write this kind of idiocy," Caryn argued, holding on to the phone with a white-knuckled grip.

"What do you mean you had no idea?" he shouted over the line. "This article says you don't know what you're doing, and I'll be honest with you, girl, I'm beginning to think the same thing."

She counted to ten in her head. "Mr. Gregory, I can't stop the way you think, but I would hope you know me well enough by now to know I'm doing the best I can. Mr. Russell feels he has a strong lead, and I understand he was going to discuss it with the police."

Mr. Gregory gave his own view of police. "Tell him to get his butt out there and just do it, or he'll be on the street with you!" He slammed the phone down.

Caryn replaced her own receiver carefully for fear she'd give in and throw it across the room.

"I wish I had told him what he could do with the job," she muttered. "Pat! I want that newspaper, now."

Pat walked in and handed her the newspaper. "Page six, second column."

Caryn read the article, feeling despair with each word. "No wonder he blew a fuse," she said quietly. "Do you know a copy of this article was express mailed to Mr. Gregory?"

"Caryn, it's not your fault," Pat insisted. "From the beginning, all you've tried to do is your job. Don't let this throw you."

Her eyes blazed. "Believe me, I don't intend to. If Sam doesn't do something about this right away I will, because I don't intend to get another call like this last one again."

"What kind of call?" Sam strolled in and sat in the chair, seemingly oblivious to the tension to the room.

Caryn held up the newspaper. "You knew about this, didn't you?"

"Not until I got in this morning." His gaze was steady.

She glanced at her watch. "Which was what? Two hours ago? Then why didn't someone tell me about it?" She stared at Pat with accusing eyes. "That way I could have been prepared when Mr. Gregory made one of his famous calls."

Sam exhaled a deep breath. "He knows?"

"Knows? He has a copy of the damn article!" By now Caryn was running full steam. "Don't worry, you weren't forgotten. If this isn't cleared up immediately we'll both be spending time in the unemployment office. I don't know about you, but that's certainly an incentive to get this taken care of now."

"Barbara stopped by the newspaper office," he went on as if she hadn't spoken. "Naturally the reporter won't give out her source and keeps citing the First Amendment. But she did drop the hint that the source worked in the building. Wonderful, huh? What, a couple thousand employees?"

Caryn stared daggers at him. "And that's supposed to make me feel better? Perhaps if you'd spend more time working than—" She stopped, horrified where her tirade was leading her.

Sam stood up, nothing of his thoughts written on his face. "Right." He turned and walked out of the office.

"Good going, Caryn," Pat said quietly.

Caryn looked up.

"You weren't sick yesterday, were you? And Sam wasn't on the road chasing a lead, either. You two finally got together and you just blew it." She refused to mince words even if the person she was yelling at was her boss. "Oh, Caryn, he cares about you. That's been evident from practically the beginning. Why couldn't you see it?"

"I did," she whispered, anguish written on her face. "We're still too different to make a go of anything."

Pat shook her head. "Then you're more stupid than I thought."

Caryn couldn't remember a day passing more slowly or her accomplishing so little work during those hours. She spent her lunch hour at the health club hoping a workout would purge her body of the tension, but even that didn't help.

When she arrived home that evening she noticed a light on in Sam's living room. She dropped her briefcase on the couch, and without bothering to change, she walked out her front door and across the concrete walk. When he didn't answer the door bell, she shrugged, held her finger pressed against the button and just allowed it to ring.

"Okay, okay." He threw open the door and scowled when he saw his visitor. "If you don't mind I'm busy trying to find the guy who's screwing up your precious magazine." He turned away preparing to close the door.

Caryn grabbed hold of the door. "Please, let me come in." Her eyes echoed her whispered plea.

Sam nodded slowly and stepped back.

Caryn followed him into the living room and sat on the edge of the couch. "I was out of line today. I was taking my anger out on you, and that wasn't fair." She took a deep breath. "You've done so much legwork on this, and I didn't even bother to acknowledge it. I'm allowing the pressure to get to me, which isn't good at all. So basically, all I can say is that I'm sorry and I hope you'll forgive my outburst." She stood, ready to leave.

"You've got some temper." Sam stood in front of her, his hands braced on his hips.

She nodded. "I've been known for it, yes."

"I thought seriously about switching your salad dressing with hot fudge sauce."

Her eyes reflected the hope that he'd forgiven her. "That sounds absolutely revolting."

"I don't know. The hot fudge sounds like it's the best part."

"I'm not very good with apologies," she said hesitantly. "I never have been."

A tiny glimmer of a smile lifted his lips. "Neither am I. I'd say that makes us a good pair."

"Are we?"

"Are we what?"

"Still a good pair?"

Sam held out his arms and Caryn went into them without a moment's hesitation. "Just because you yelled at me today and I was ready to throttle you didn't mean I stopped loving you," he murmured, then drew back. "But you thought that, didn't you? Why?"

She shook her head, not wanting to disturb the closeness between them.

His hand found her nape and massaged the taut skin. "Why, Caryn? Was it your father?" His tone was as gentle as his touch. "Is that what he used to do with you? Blackmail you with his love if you lost a race or something?" The stiffness in her body told him the truth. His softly spoken words about her father were far from kind.

"He didn't know any other way, Sam." She still made excuses for her father. "He wanted the three of us to be the best, and when we won he was happy."

"And when you lost he wasn't." He pulled back a little and gently shook her shoulders. "Caryn, love is unconditional. Hey, you could grow a wart on your nose tomorrow and I'd still love you. I'd find you the best dermatologist in town, but I'd still love you."

Her smile appeared, but her eyes were a bit watery as she wondered what she had done to deserve someone so special. "That's very comforting."

Sam pulled her back into his embrace, wishing he could keep her there forever. "Did you eat any dinner? And don't lie to me," he warned.

"I came here right away."

He nodded. "Okay, let's see what we can find for you in the kitchen. Don't worry, I have healthy food in there, too. Do you have any important work that needs to be done?"

Caryn nodded. "A couple of articles to be proofed."

"Why don't you bring them over here. I promise to stay out of your way until you're finished. But then I expect to be rewarded for leaving you alone. Sound fair?" Keeping an arm draped around her shoulders, he guided her into the kitchen and sat her down while he rummaged in the refrigerator. "Aha, a couple of chicken breasts. Those are safe to eat, right?"

"Very safe." Caryn insisted on going through his cabinets looking for seasoning, and was pleased she could even find some. After the chicken was seasoned she put the breasts under the broiler. "As for your idea—it's very tempting, except for one thing."

Sam held his breath, fearing he was about to receive a very polite rejection, and his mind already whirled with ideas on how to change her mind. "What's that?"

She looked a little sheepish. "Your bed tends to make me feel just a little bit seasick."

He nodded, the relief flowing through him. "No problem there. Either I buy you some Dramamine, which would probably put you to sleep, or we use your place. I don't know about you, but I vote for the latter."

Chapter Fifteen

"Earth to Russell. Earth to Russell. Come in, Russell." Brian leaned across the desk and snapped his fingers in front of his boss's face.

Sam blinked his eyes and smiled. "Are you trying to tell me something?"

"For the past two weeks you haven't walked with mortal man," he replied, leaning back in his chair placing his fingers together in a steeple shape. "Am I to guess that you and the invincible Ms. Richards are an item?"

"Because I'm not always among the land of the living?" he said lightly, drawing deeply on his cigarette.

"You go off into a trance at odd times, you're smoking more, and there are times your temper isn't the coolest," he pointed out. "And when you and Caryn are together, you both take great pains not to look at each other."

"You'd make a good detective," Sam said sarcastically.

"It doesn't take a detective to tell there's more to the two of you than meets the eye." Brian pushed himself out of his chair. "Well, I'm off."

Once alone, Sam thought over the past fifteen days. Had his preoccupation with Caryn shown that much? So why wasn't he surprised?

Since that first night they spent at Caryn's place they had spent almost every evening together. And each time Sam grew more and more bothered. Because most of those nights he would wake up a few hours later and discover Caryn wasn't lying next to him. The first time it happened and he noticed a light shining from downstairs, he was tempted to get up and see if there was anything wrong, but something held him back. Each time it happened he still thought about seeking her out and each time he held back. He often wondered why he didn't ask her about her nocturnal activities.

"The time will come," he muttered, stubbing out his cigarette and immediately lighting another, "at least when everything else is straightened out." He picked up the phone and called downstairs, asking to speak to Caryn. His voice softened when she came on the line. "Hi."

"Is this another one of your obscene calls?" she asked, her voice even more husky. "The last one had me desiring a cold shower."

Sam chuckled. "You were supposed to desire me, not a shower."

"Sorry, my dear, but during working hours I have to concentrate on something other than your sexual fantasies."

"I don't know. I thought the last one was pretty good." He stared at the target he had set up on the opposite wall for his rubber-band gun. The reason for his call tapped at his memory. "I only wish that was why I called. Things have been quiet for too long."

"Calm before the storm."

"Exactly." He leaned back in his chair and propped his feet on top of his desk. "I've thought about this for a while and I think our best bet is to set a trap."

"With me as the bait," she murmured.

"No, but with something that concerns you. Especially if our little prankster thinks it could mean your job. Do you have any ideas?" He eyed the glowing tip of his cigarette.

"Give me a little while and I'll come up with something," she promised. "Sam, I have to go. I have a meeting in a few minutes. Also, get rid of the cigarette." She hung up.

Sam stared at his cigarette, then the phone, then back to the cigarette. "How does she do it?"

PAT STUCK HER HEAD IN. "Everything okay?"

Caryn shrugged. "Come in and close the door." She waited until the secretary had stepped inside and shut the door behind her. "Were the offices checked today?"

Pat nodded. "First thing this morning. I have to admit when Sam first came up with the idea that the offices might be bugged I thought he was a bit off base."

"Until that expert he had come in found the bugs under the desk." Caryn finished. "This has gotten so sick. Sam called because he wants to set a trap. He thinks it's been too long between episodes, and I think he's afraid the next one could be very dangerous. Not to mention Mr. Gregory wants this stopped within the week." She sighed.

Pat shuddered. "Why is it when everything is going great out here he leaves us alone, but the minute we have problems he's poking his nose in, acting as if he knows exactly how to handle it."

Caryn smiled wryly. "Especially when he doesn't bother to gather all the facts first. Oh yes, our illustrious leader and world-class tyrant certainly knows how to put the fear into his people. It's a good thing he pays all of us so well. Otherwise the threat of losing our jobs wouldn't frighten us so much."

Pat examined her nails, which she'd had manicured during her lunch hour. "You and Sam have become pretty close over the past few weeks."

"Oh, I wouldn't say that," Caryn said a bit too casually, hoping she wasn't blushing.

"None of us are blind, Caryn. The vibrations between the two of you are so strong we almost get knocked off our chairs. Besides, he's turned you into a new person. I just want you to know that you have our blessing." Pat smiled.

"That's very comforting to know," she said dryly.

Caryn hadn't bothered to confirm everyone's wild guesses where she and Sam were concerned, because she preferred keeping their relationship to herself. Even then, just thinking about the hours they spent together warmed her blood. Other thoughts also cropped up.

"Pat, do you honestly think I'm a new person?" Caryn asked hesitantly.

"New? You're positively glowing, and we both know the reason why," she enthused. "I like the new you, Caryn. Not to say there was anything wrong with the old person. It's just that you're a bit softer, more approachable. Sam's good for you. Don't let him get away."

She felt a tightness in her chest. "Sometimes we don't have any choice in that department. If the man wants to leave."

"I think if Sam had his way he'd be surgically grafted to your side," Pat added. "No, I don't think you have anything to worry about." She left the office, softly closing the door behind her.

"If I have nothing to worry about why do I still feel so apprehensive?" she whispered, feeling the old panic well up in her chest.

"WHERE HAVE YOU BEEN?" Sam stood in the open doorway of Caryn's house, hands on hips, face looking angrier than she had ever seen it.

"I had some thinking to do," Caryn muttered, trying to pass by him, but he refused to move. "How did you get in?"

"You gave me a key, remember? And don't try to get me off the subject." Sam stepped back and followed her up the stairs, not allowing her to escape. "If you needed to think, why are you dressed in your sweats, looking as if you just ran the Los Angeles Marathon?"

"I told you before, running helps me clear my head," she said tautly, stalking through her bedroom and into the bathroom, pulling her sweatshirt over her head and tossing it in the hamper before leaning over to take off her shoes and socks. She looked up, seeing Sam standing just inside the room. "Do you mind? I'd like to take a shower."

"My being here has never stopped you before."

"What is so wrong with having some privacy!" Caryn jerked off her pants and threw them into the hamper, slamming the lid down. "I swear every time I turn around you're looking over my shoulder. If I didn't know better I would think I was the criminal!" She stomped over to the shower and twisted the faucets. She spun around, staring at Sam who looked back at her with no emotion stamped on his features. Without saying a word, he backed away and closed the door.

Caryn got under the strong spray fighting the urge to burst into tears. For someone who had always held her emotions in check, she felt as if they were all drowning her at once, and she didn't know how to handle the deluge. She stepped directly under the spray allowing it to flow over her face and hair. She had no idea how long she stood under the water, only that she felt a great deal calmer when she finished. Combing her wet hair behind her ears, she then used dusting powder and lotion on her body before tucking a towel around herself. When she opened the door she was surprised to find Sam lounging on her bed reading a magazine. He turned his head at her entrance.

"You thought I'd be gone, didn't you?" he asked quietly, watching her cross the room to the closet and open it to look for a robe.

"I wouldn't have been surprised."

"Is that what you wanted? To be left alone tonight? Or did you want to be left alone from now on?"

Caryn's hand froze as it reached for a robe. Her actions were slow as she wrapped the robe around her and zipped it up before turning to face him. "Tell me the truth. Don't you feel as if everything between us is going too fast?"

"No," he said without hesitation. "But obviously you do."

She shook her head, wishing she hadn't spoken so impulsively. "First we were business associates, then we were neighbors, friends, then lovers. Now we're almost living together. You have an extra razor in my bathroom."

"And you're worried about the next step," Sam guessed. "That's logical, and you've always been a logical woman, haven't you?" He patted the spot next to him. "Come here." His lips twisted when he noticed her hesitation. "Don't worry, I don't intend to seduce you into submission."

Caryn walked slowly over to the bed and sat on the edge. He reached out and drew her back until she lay next to him. She closed her eyes, preferring not to look at his face. He did nothing more than keep an arm around her shoulders as she laid her head on his shoulder.

"You're scared," he said softly. "You're scared I'm going to run out on you the way your ex-fiancé did."

"You don't know what happened between us," she said tightly.

"No, but I can guess, and you probably started freezing him off the way you tried with me tonight. The difference is, I can see through your little game." He spoke in the same abstracted voice he used when he discussed his work with her. "Obviously he didn't care enough to do the same. If you think I'm too harsh with my conclusions I won't apologize. You can act like the world's worst shrew, but you're not going to scare me off." He turned on his side and looked down into her face that resembled a pale mask. "I'm in here for the duration, my love."

Caryn opened her eyes and looked seriously at Sam. "Don't make any promises you can't keep." She closed them again and turned her face away.

If it had been any other woman Sam would have gotten off the bed and walked out the door without a backward glance. But that was before he had met and fallen in love with Caryn.

"I THOUGHT YOU WANTED to set a trap." Caryn paced from one end of Sam's office to the other.

He watched her from his favorite position, his body sprawled in his chair and feet propped on top of his desk. "I wanted to set a trap, but not with you as bait. I said that already. I don't want you in any more danger. Didn't that football game at the park give you any indication what this person wants to do to you?"

She spun around, strands of her hair caressing her cheek. "Is that why you've been spending so much time with me? Have you taken on bodyguard duties also?"

Sam uncoiled himself from his chair and slowly advanced on her. Caryn didn't move a muscle, only lifted her head in a gesture of defiance. When he reached her, he placed one hand on either side of the wall, effectively imprisoning her.

"You are working very hard to toss me out of your life by goading me into doing the walking out," he said quietly, with a voice as hard as steel. "Now I don't know what the problem is, but I'm more than willing to listen to anything you have to say, as long as it has to do with what's going on in that crazy brain of yours." She stiffened in his embrace although she made no effort to try to leave him.

"You have a vivid imagination."

"And you are asking for it. Now—" he looked at his watch "—I have an appointment in ten minutes, and as much as I'd like to get this settled between us, I don't think it can be done in that short a period of time. If you want to give me more ideas for a trap, fine, but nothing where you're concerned. Understand? Otherwise, I'll talk to the others on my staff and come up with something else. Even with the way you've been acting lately I'd still like to have you in one piece." Before Caryn could say a word Sam's mouth covered hers in a deep kiss that stole her breath. He made no move to touch her further, other than his lips moving over hers with strong possession. When he finally drew away both of them were breathing heavily.

"If you don't use me as bait, the plan will never work," she said quietly, before slipping under his upraised arm and leaving the office.

Sam looked at the closed door. "Why can't she be wrong once in a while?" he muttered darkly.

Caryn wasn't about to stop even with Sam's orders to stay out of it. She arranged for everyone to meet at a nearby restaurant for lunch the next day where she could discuss her plan.

"Dr. Milford's first two articles just came in." Tami walked into Caryn's office.

"How do they look?"

"Very impressive." She sat down and crossed her legs, which hiked her dark brown leather skirt even higher. Her dark gold turtleneck sweater highlighted her exotic coloring, and her chocolate-brown wide leather belt accentuated her slim waist. "One deals with eating disorders in general, explaining what they are, warning signs, and what can eventually happen. The other talks about teen stress and how to cope with it. I'd really like to run that one first since our teen issue is coming up soon. It would be perfect for it."

Caryn nodded. "Sounds good to me."

Tami paused. "Do you think our practical joker has stopped?"

"Do you mean has he taken a vacation?" She shook her head, smiling sadly. "One of my fears is that he's just laying low for a while waiting for me to grow complacent, and then strike."

"You're not going to take this lying down, are you?"

"Absolutely not," Caryn said firmly. "That's why I want all of us to get together tomorrow to discuss a plan of our own."

"Does Sam know about this?"

"There's no reason for him to know. This is our problem."

"Okay, I just hope you know what you're doing, because if Sam finds out he's going to be very ticked off." Tami stood up.

"Look at it this way. If this all blows up in my face you'll have an excellent chance of getting my job," Caryn said lightly.

"If this blows up we'll all be out of a job," she predicted.

"I FEEL AS IF I'm in a mystery movie by saying 'I'm sure you all are wondering why I brought you here,'" Caryn told the assembled group in the private dining area they had taken over for the lunch hour.

"Are you paying for lunch?" Jay asked, then ducked the wadded-up napkins thrown his way.

"Tacky, Jay, very tacky," Lee drawled.

"Honestly, Jay, have you no manners?" Jodi chipped in. "You wait long enough and Caryn will pick up the bill." She grinned at her boss.

"Actually—" Caryn's eyes danced with wicked laughter "—Mr. Gregory is paying for this luncheon. Since this concerns the magazine the bill's going on my expense report, so order to your little heart's content." Everyone applauded.

"Do they have lobster here?" Janna asked.

"How about caviar?"

"All right, what's going on?" Lee asked, once they all had ordered their meals.

"Besides what Tami told you?"

"All I said was that you wanted to discuss our prankster and that Sam wasn't invited," she defended herself.

Caryn shifted in her seat, feeling uneasy and just a little bit guilty. She hadn't expected his name to be brought up. Especially not since he had called not more than ten minutes before she left the office to see if she wanted to meet him for lunch. She explained to him she had a business appointment and would see him that evening. By the time her salad arrived she had no appetite.

"So, oh fearless leader, what is your nefarious plan?" Jay asked, once they had finished eating.

"When did you start reading the dictionary?" Lee asked him. "Correction, who read it to you?"

Caryn stood, holding her hands up, indicating silence. "Children, no fighting please. We have plans to make."

"Tin cans tied to a string tied across doorways?" Tami asked. "We could also try that bucket trick. It was effective with you. Maybe a couple of exploding light bulbs."

"That was the first trick played on us," Jodi reminded her. "Why can't we set up remote cameras to see who comes in and out?"

"Mr. Gregory refuses to have any more money spent on high tech. The offices won't be swept for bugs after Friday," Caryn explained. "That's why I tried to come up with something simple and, hopefully, effective."

"Such as?" Lee asked.

Caryn leaned forward. "Since I'm the victim I have to be the bait." She shushed the loud protests. "What I want us to do is set something up that hopefully gets picked up and acted upon. We need to let the word out that we have some very important articles—an exposé on a fitness company, something like that. And I'll be working late one night on the article. With luck, the person will show up."

"And we hide behind our desks and jump out yelling 'surprise'?" Tami asked, sarcasm in her tone. "Caryn, it won't work."

"It will," she insisted. "All it needs is a bit of fine tuning, and some help from you."

"What do you want us to do?" Jay asked.

Caryn shot him a grateful glance. "One thing Tami is right about. I don't want to stay in the offices alone. It will have to look as if you've all left the offices. You have to somehow sneak back in without anyone seeing you."

Within minutes everyone was tossing ideas back and forth, except for Tami, who sat back, her arms crossed in front of her chest. She and Caryn stared at each other across the table, neither one listening to the talk floating around them.

"If Sam finds out about this he'll murder you himself," Tami said quietly.

"Then I suggest you not say anything to him," Caryn said just as quietly.

By the time they left the restaurant they had what they felt was a well-thought-out plan and tentatively set the day for the following Tuesday evening.

"It'll work," Jay pronounced.

"I hope so," Caryn sighed.

"WHAT DO YOU THINK you're trying to do?" Sam ranted, pacing back and forth. "Tell me something, do you think you were reincarnated as one of Charlie's Angels?"

"You already used that phrase," she said wearily. Curled up on a corner of the couch, Caryn had been watching and listening to Sam for the past hour.

"I don't want to hear any sarcasm," he practically snarled, skidding to a stop in front of her. "Do you realize what could happen if this backfires on you? You could end up seriously hurt. Doesn't that matter to you? What about me? Do you think I'd want to get the news of your lying in a hospital bed, or worse, in a morgue? We have no idea what this person is like. Anything could happen!"

Caryn looked more self-assured than she felt. Once Sam began tearing her plan to pieces she realized just how many holes there were in it.

"I'm just tired of waiting for something to happen and then get blamed for something that isn't my fault!" she burst out, dropping her head back and staring up at the ceiling. "I want this all over with, Sam. And if you can't do something about it, I will."

He squatted down in front of her and took her hands, absently noticing how cold her skin was. "Caryn your plan has merit."

"At least I did something right." Bitterness laced her voice.

He squeezed her hands. "It's just that amateurs can screw up even the best of plans. Have you considered that someone else could get hurt?"

Her head snapped upward, eyes wide. "But I'm the bait. Why would one of the others be in danger?"

"Because they would be interfering with what is obviously the main objective—getting even with you," he stated, rubbing her hands with his fingers and bringing one up to his lips. "I know you've seen me take this slow, but I'm also playing it safe. I don't want anyone to get hurt, especially you."

"You can say that after all I've done to you lately?"

His lips twisted. "Protecting you is part of my job." He ducked her playfully upraised fist. "Ignoring your little tantrums isn't in my job description, but I'll put them down to a bout of PMS."

"I don't suffer from PMS," she gritted.

"There's always a first time." Sam's expression turned serious. "Forget your plan, Caryn, or so help me I'll put a full-time guard on those office doors."

"Why hasn't there been one before?"

"Because I want to catch the guy. A guard will only put him off. Without catching the culprit, we can't find out who hired him."

"You once said you thought it was an inside job," Caryn brought up.

He nodded. "And I still do. In fact, I think it's your janitor, but so far I have no proof. Lieutenant Kendall even checked him out for me, and the guy's record is squeaky clean."

"Larry?" She shook her head with disbelief. "No, not him. He's worked in the building for years. He's so honest it's almost a joke. Pat once accidentally tossed an envelope in the wastebasket that had fifty dollars in it. The money fell out, and Larry found it, promptly returning it to her. He could have kept it, and she wouldn't have been the wiser. No, I can't believe it might be him. Accuse someone else."

"It doesn't work that way, honey," he said gently. "I feel very strongly it's him, and if so, he's been very clever setting everything up. I want to catch him, Caryn. I want it so bad I can taste it."

She looked him square in the eye. "I want to be in on this, Sam. You have your hunches and I have mine. You won't catch him unless I'm part of it."

His expression turned grim. "No way."

"I won't let up on this," she warned.

"No."

Caryn leaned forward and slipped her arms around his neck. She tipped her head to one side and angled her mouth across his. "I'll make it worth your while," she murmured, tracing the shape with her tongue.

"Your seducing me won't accomplish a thing," he muttered.

She ran her hands down his back and around his jeans waistband, her touch light but arousing. "Not a thing?"

"I won't let you get involved in this." His resolve was wavering and he hated himself for it. With a groan issued from deep in his throat, he pushed her away none too gently. "Don't treat what we have so cheaply that you'd use it to gain your objective," he said harshly, straightening up and walking away, raking his fingers through his hair. "Damn, I need a cigarette."

Caryn felt the shame race through her body at his words. "Oh, Sam, I'm so sorry. I wouldn't hurt you for anything. I love you."

He spun around, all motion arrested. "What did you say?"

She bit her lower lip. "I've felt that way for a long time, but I've been afraid to say it. I just want you to know I didn't want to cause dissension between us. It's just that I'm so scared." Tears pricked her eyelids.

Sam swiftly returned to her. When Caryn stood up she immediately went into his arms.

"I don't want to fight with you." Her words were muffled against his shirt front.

He chuckled. "I don't know, you used to enjoy it not all that long ago."

"That was different."

"Why?" He nuzzled her neck.

"You weren't my lover then. I was fighting my attraction to you. Now, I just want to make love with you." Her fingers gripped his belt.

"They say the best part of fighting is making up. Shall we find out?" He buried his face in the scented skin visible above the scoop neck of her blue top while one hand insinuated itself under the hem.

"Just a minute." She pushed him away. Her eyes were narrowed with suspicion as she gazed at him. "Who was the snitch?"

He tried not to laugh. "The snitch? Oh, Caryn, you do like detective novels, don't you?"

"It was Tami, wasn't it?" she demanded. "She wasn't for this in the beginning. I should have known she wouldn't keep her word."

"Such as in not telling me?" Caryn's flushed face gave him his answer, except now his anger was replaced by amusement. "Then rest assured she didn't."

"Then who did?"

Sam grinned. "Brian."

Her brow furrowed. "Brian? How did he know?"

His grin grew even wider. "Tami told him."

Chapter Sixteen

"You were right about my father. He did use his love as a tool to get us to do better." Caryn's words floated in the darkness.

Sam turned over on his side and remained silent as he sensed she had more to say. Instead he lay there listening to her breathing.

"Dad always told us we were to be the best in everything we did," she went on, staring up at the ceiling. "When I won a race he told the world he knew I could do it and how proud he was of me. When I lost he pointed out all the mistakes I made and why I let the other kid beat me. Second wasn't good enough for him and third was the same as coming in last. I was in training from the age of six until college. I remember one time when I was nine he drove by while I was walking home from school. Unfortunately I was eating a candy bar. He stopped the car, took the candy bar away and told me I wasn't allowed to watch TV for two weeks." Her voice was tinged with sorrow. "I was only nine, Sam. At nine, you lost privileges because you didn't clean up your room or you flunked a test. Not because you were caught with a candy bar."

"Did your mother ever say anything during all this?"

"What could she say? Dad's word was law in our household. Actually, Mom ran the house and Dad ran us." A tear ran down her cheek, visible in the moonlight coming through the window and falling across the bed. "When Cam and Scott grew interested in girls they had it really rough, because they had strict curfews on Friday nights when they had a game or track meet the next day. Scott once sneaked out one night to keep a date with a girl he had lusted after for three months before she finally agreed to go out with him," she said softly. "Dad found out and Scott didn't have his car for the rest of the school year."

Sam reached over and grasped her hand. "And what about you? Did you have the strict curfews when all you wanted to do was chase boys?"

Caryn nodded. "Mine were even worse, because Dad didn't trust the boys. Pretty soon the boys were afraid to ask me out. Especially if they were going to attend the university where Dad would be their coach."

"If there were so many restrictions how come your brothers went into sports? If it had been me I would have been turned off them for the rest of my life."

She inched over until she was lying close to him. Sensing she needed comfort, he put his arms around her. "Because they sincerely loved sports and they tended to ignore Dad when he was on the rampage. They were better off than I was," she said simply.

"But you couldn't ignore him?" he guessed.

"No." Caryn sighed, rolling over until her face was cradled by the indentation between Sam's shoulder and neck.

"Is that why you love me? Because I'm the exact opposite of what your father would want for you?" he questioned, rubbing the tense muscles of her nape.

"No, never. My rebellion was getting away from sports as a business," she replied. "As you once said, you grew on me."

His hands carefully inched their way around to the front. The soft silky fabric of her nightgown slid under his palms. "So it was my sexy charm and not because I tend to eat too much fast food and pretend to be asleep on the mornings you go out running that got to you."

She smiled. "I knew you were faking."

His palms found the peaked nipples and rubbed them sensuously. "Oh, how?"

"You only snore when you're pretending to be asleep." Her breath warmed his jaw.

"We're not finished with this, you know," he whispered.

Caryn sighed and moved away, flopping onto her back. "Sam, I just told you more than I've ever told anyone. I think we're more than finished with the subject."

"What was the real reason you gave up sports? And don't tell me it was because you found journalism more interesting than running." He tapped the end of her nose.

"I do believe this is Sam Russell, the investigator, now talking," she groaned.

"You're right. So don't lie to me, Caryn. I'll be able to tell."

She drew a deep breath and recited in a monotone, "I quit sports because I was tired of the strict curfews, of not having fun on the weekends—"

"Try again."

Caryn tossed her head back and forth on the pillow. "Obviously you've never been faced with a training table, and you think I don't eat a lot now. You should have seen me then.''

"Caryn, stop it!" Sam's voice lashed out through the darkness. "I told you not to fool with me. I want to know."

"Why?"

"Because I love you, and whatever happened in the past still affects the way you consider me. Look how long it took you to admit you loved me. And you still fear I'm going to walk out on you or not love you for some imagined wrong."

She stiffened. "I already told you. My father used his love as a bargaining tool to keep us in line. We were to be winners for him. The only trouble was the boys had an easier time of it than I did. They truly enjoyed competing. I didn't."

He frowned. "Why not? You certainly seem to enjoy competing in the business world."

"You're not dealing with kids then." She rolled over on her side, now fully prepared to explain it to him. "When kids are training with the Olympics in sight, they have to be so focused in one area that they can't allow for anything else to enter their lives. They have that one goal and that's all they can see. I wanted too many other things."

"And wanting more left you dissatisfied," he guessed.

"Yes. I finally realized that there had to be more to life than sports. I was good, but I didn't have that dedication needed to go that extra mile. I liked running and I was good in competition, but I wasn't good enough. It upset my father more than it did me, and I don't think he's ever forgiven me for it," she murmured sadly.

"Did you ever discuss it with him? Tell him exactly how you felt about all this and why you weren't right for competition?" Sam asked, thinking of the many good-natured battles he had indulged in with his own father.

She shook her head. "That is a subject that isn't brought up. So now, we see each other a few times a year, and if we're lucky we don't get into a fight where my mother has to intervene."

"How does your mother feel about this? I can't believe she's so weak-willed she would have allowed this to go on."

Caryn chuckled as she reached over, placing her hand on his chest, desperately needing that contact. As she spoke, her fingers combed the rough thatch of hair. "Believe me, the last person you would call weak-willed is my mother. If you're smart you'll never have her in your house, especially your bathroom. She's always telling me how my bath towels are a disgrace. She loves to redecorate bathrooms. As for the other, she wished she had intervened earlier in my life after she realized how I felt. You see, I never let on how I really felt about sports, so she had no idea. We talked about it about a year ago."

"You certainly do keep things in, don't you?" Sam muttered, covering her wandering hand with his. "Oh, Caryn, what am I going to do with you?"

She leaned over him, her hand slowly moving downward. "Since I've purged my soul perhaps you should do what you do best. Love me. But I think this is one time that the loving should be on me."

"I, ah, I won't argue there," he said hoarsely.

Caryn brushed her lips across his, then nipped his chin. She nibbled her way along his jaw and down his throat until she reached the more vulnerable area of his neck.

"You smell like my peppermint soap," she murmured against his skin. "Mmm, I love candy canes at Christmas. They always taste so fresh." Her tongue darted out for a quick taste.

Sam gasped. "If you keep this up I could lose my sanity."

"Shall I stop?" Caryn breathed against a rock-hard nipple. Then her teeth fastened on the tiny nub.

"No!"

Laughing throatily, Caryn continued her slow and sure seduction of Sam. By the time she completed their union he was ready to scream with frustration. It wasn't long before they both climaxed.

"You really know how to drive a guy crazy," Sam gasped, pushing Caryn's damp hair away from her face.

"You crazy? I'm the one who was ready to go over the edge," she argued amiably.

"Yes, but you were in charge. I'm just glad you put me out of my misery."

Caryn lifted her head, her lips curved in a broad smile. "It was entirely my pleasure."

"NO, ABSOLUTELY NOT!" Sam picked up and drank his breakfast coffee, his face set in grim lines. "And I don't want to hear any more about it."

"Why not?" Caryn leaned across the kitchen table and gripped his arm. "If you were in charge we would have a chance and you know it."

He set his cup down and stared at her long and hard. "What you are proposing is dangerous and I don't intend to have something happen to you."

"Neither do I. Sam, I trust you. If anyone will keep me safe it's you. I'm not afraid," she said.

"Well, I am," he said roughly, picking up his coffee cup again. "Caryn, this isn't some kind of joke. This is serious business. Didn't that football game mean anything to you?" His eyes were dark with the memory.

She recalled the pain. "Yes, it did. That's why I want to do something before it's done to me. Now, are you willing? Because if you aren't I'll go ahead with it on my own," she added on a reckless note.

Sam studied her for a long moment. "Okay, let's get on with it. I don't want our talk to leave this room until I speak to my own people, and I'll be in complete charge."

Caryn nodded, smiling now that Sam had finally given in. "I'll do anything you say."

He sighed heavily. "Why am I having trouble with that statement?"

ONCE SAM AND CARYN had discussed all the pros and cons, even though they didn't always agree with each other's views, they left for work. Sam met his own staff and went over his talk with Caryn.

Brian spoke up. "You know, she has something there. Did you tell her if she ever gets tired of the magazine she could work up here?"

Sam's look was deadly. "No."

Several men exchanged knowing glances and grins.

"So we're doing this next Tuesday night?" Chad asked. "Is the janitor Larry working on the cleaning crew that night?"

Sam nodded. "I already checked his schedule. That was one of the points Caryn hadn't bothered to find out first. Of course she doesn't want to think it's him.''

"I learned something very interesting about the man that I'm still wondering why we didn't pick up on before," Barbara said. "Did you know his wife is in a nursing home?" She looked smug at catching them off guard as they turned toward her, their interest now pricked. "Obviously you didn't know."

"Nursing homes can be very expensive," Sam mused.

Barbara sobered. "She's suffering from Alzheimer's and needs constant care."

"He's been with the company for more than twenty years. Why would he do it?" Chad asked. "Wouldn't the group insurance cover this?"

"Insurance payments for constant care for such a prolonged period would only run out after a while."

"And money talks," one of the other men said quietly.

"All right, we'll draft out this plan on paper and smooth out all the bugs," Sam announced. "With luck this will be all over by Tuesday. I hope," he muttered under his breath.

"ARE YOU NERVOUS?" Sam asked Caryn when they met for lunch on D-day.

"Yes," she confessed, toying with her salad fork.

"There's nothing wrong with that," he assured her. "I just want you to know that if you don't want to go through with it, you don't have to."

She straightened her spine. "I won't back down now."

Sam nodded. "Fine. You and Tami are to start your battle at three. Larry's going to be called up there by Lori for some problem. Hopefully he'll take the bait."

Caryn managed a stiff smile. "Hopefully."

A few minutes before three Tami walked into Caryn's office and offered her boss a brief smile.

"Is Lori going to buzz you when he comes in?" she asked, standing just inside the door.

She nodded. "We then wait another minute or so before we begin, to give him time to come back here."

"Caryn, what if Sam is wrong? What if it isn't Larry?"

Caryn didn't look happy at the prospect, after all the evidence Sam had laid before her at lunch. "Then we'll just have to wait until our avenger strikes again. And I don't want to do that. This waiting has been worst." They both started in surprise when Caryn's intercom buzzed. The two women stared at each other for a moment, then Tami opened her mouth and took a deep breath.

"Caryn, we can't have that lying around!" she shouted. "This is our most important issue to date. That article in there is an exclusive and he didn't even want me to make a copy. If something happens to the article and pictures we're going to be in a lot of trouble. *You're* going to be in a lot of trouble," Tami said loudly.

"As I'm the one in charge here I think I should be the one to worry about it, not you," Caryn retorted just as loudly. "It will be perfectly safe in my office, because I'll have the door locked. So you see, there isn't anything for you to worry about."

"The way you keep screwing things up you may not be in charge here much longer," Tami argued forcefully. "If you aren't going to listen to me let's see if Mr. Gregory will agree with me about the shoddy way you're handling things." She spun around and stormed out of the room and past Pat's desk, where Larry stood looking uncertain.

"I, ah, I'm sorry, Ms. Richards," he mumbled, shifting from one foot to the other. "I got a call saying you were having trouble with your office door."

"Oh, yes, Larry, it appears to be sticking. I'm glad you could come up so promptly." Caryn mustered up a smile. She still couldn't believe that Sam felt this colorless, shy man was the culprit. And she refused to believe he would try to harm her.

He didn't look at her directly. "I'll see what I can do."

Caryn left the mock articles and pictures on her desk and purposely stepped out of her office for about ten minutes. During that time she holed up in Lee's office, pacing back and forth and wringing her hands.

"I almost hope Sam's right, so it will all be over," she told the other woman.

Lee looked at her with sympathy. "I can't say I blame you there."

When Caryn returned to her office Larry was gone, and a glance at her desk indicated the papers had been moved. She put a call in to Sam.

"It appears you were right. The papers aren't in the same place."

"All right, you've done your part. Just go home at your usual time. I don't want anyone staying late tonight, especially you," he said.

"I want to be in on this," she argued. "When I first brought it up I intended to be here."

"Caryn, please do as I say," he said wearily. "As soon as everything is settled I'll call you." He wasn't surprised that she hung up on him, just as he knew deep down that she wouldn't let the situation rest.

Early that evening Lieutenant Kendall appeared in Sam's office.

"You really like to take the law into your own hands, don't you?" he said mildly.

"I'm just relieved that I found out Caryn's crazy scheme in time. Who knows what would have happened if I hadn't." Sam loosened his tie and lit a cigarette.

"I hope you'll remember that I'll be the one to do the arresting," the detective said.

Sam grinned. "You guys always get the glamour work."

"Sam?" Chad stuck his head around the door. "Jeff just called to tell us Larry finished his cleaning in the *Simple Fitness* offices, and it appears he left the front door unlocked."

The two men's eyes met.

"It looks like this is it," Lieutenant Kendall said quietly.

Sam sighed. "Yeah. So why don't I feel happy about it? We have a comfortable spot waiting for us in the stairwell. Ready?"

CARYN REMAINED QUIET in a corner of the darkroom until she heard Larry leave. She crept out into the studio, relieved that the lights from the outside were enough to enable her to see her way without bumping into something. She opened the door a crack, which allowed her to see the hallway and, she hoped, remain unseen. She had no idea how long she stood there before a whispering sound was heard from the front. She tensed when a large shadow seemed to materialize before her, moving silently down the hallway. She held her breath until she heard scratching sounds. Slowly opening the door, she slipped out, keeping close to the wall as she noticed her previously locked door was standing open. She inched her way down the hall until she stood next to the doorway. Looking through, she could see the shadowy figure standing behind her desk. She almost gasped when he flipped open a lighter, the flame burning orange and blue.

"Wait a minute!" Caryn shouted, fearing the worst as she ran inside. "What do you think you're doing?"

The man looked up, his unfamiliar fleshy features highlighted by the flame. "Get out, lady," he growled.

She almost stepped back, but then refused to back down. "You're the one who's done all those terrible things, aren't you?"

"You must be the high-and-mighty Caryn Richards." His smile was pure evil. "Too bad my boss isn't here to see this." His arm lashed out, the flame coming dangerously close to Caryn, forcing her to jump back. "I wouldn't suggest you get too close, unless you want to get hurt."

Caryn turned cold. "You were at the park," she whispered. "You threw the rock. Your boss is Jenkins, isn't it?"

"None of your business." He withdrew a snub-nosed revolver and trained it on Caryn. "Now I suggest you just stand there very quietly. I'll get to you next."

Sam, where are you? her mind called out. *Oh, Sam, I know you're going to yell at me and be furious with me, but I don't care. Just please get here right away!*

"And I suggest you hold it right there." Lieutenant Kendall's commanding voice froze the two people.

The man seemed to debate the idea of escape, but the two men standing in the doorway with several more behind them, some in uniform, changed his mind.

"What do you think you were doing?" Sam shouted, pulling on Caryn's arm, dragging her over to a corner of the office. "Do you realize what he could have done to you?" Even as he yelled at her he pulled her into his arms and held her tight enough to almost crack her ribs. "I could throttle you for taking years off my life." His voice was muffled by her hair.

"I knew mental telepathy would work and you'd save me," she mumbled against his shirt front. "And I vowed I'd even let you yell at me."

"You're damn right I'm going to yell at you. Once we get home you're going to hear the lecture of all time. Don't you ever do this to me again, do you hear me? Otherwise I'll start locking you in the bathroom."

"Why don't you take her on home," Brian suggested, grinning at his irate boss. "Chad and I can finish up here."

Sam nodded. Larry had already been taken into custody and was tearfully explaining his part in the fiasco.

"He promised me enough money to pay for my wife's medical care," he said tearfully to the police officers. He looked at the men standing in a circle around him. "You don't know how expensive it is, even with my group insurance. He said no one would be hurt, so I wasn't to worry, just to unlock a few doors or provide the necessary keys when he wanted them. I swear to you, if I'd known what he had planned I wouldn't have gone along. It's just that I had to think of my wife. We have no other family. I wanted to make sure she would be well taken care of," he pleaded with them, his pale eyes glistening with tears.

Sam had stayed around long enough to listen to Larry's story. No matter what the man's reason he couldn't feel any sympathy for him. Instead, he returned to Caryn and hustled her downstairs to the parking garage.

"Don't you have to go to the police station or something?" she babbled, fearing his lecture was going to be much worse than she'd first thought.

"I can go in tomorrow. Tonight I'm going to make sure you never do this again." His pale eyes promised a punishment she might not appreciate. "I swear if I thought it would do any good I'd paddle your fanny until you couldn't sit down for a month."

Caryn's hands swiftly covered that portion of her anatomy.

"If I didn't love you so much I would seriously think about it," Sam muttered, quickly unlocking the car doors and pushing her into the passenger seat. "Now, we're going home and you're going to listen to every word I have to say about following orders." As he walked around the rear of the car he was still maligning her stubborn nature.

Even though Sam's anger was much more than Caryn expected she still couldn't stop smiling. When he slid behind the steering wheel she leaned over and kissed him long and hard, her tongue teasing his lips apart.

"What was that for?" Sam whispered when she finally released him.

She smiled. "That was for still loving me even though I screwed up."

"That's the problem. I love you so much I can't see straight," he said crossly.

"I have a much better punishment in mind," she whispered.

Sam looked at her suspiciously. "Such as?"

Caryn toyed with his shirt button before slowly releasing it. "Just make love to me until I can't do anything but agree to anything you say."

Sam chuckled, most of his earlier temper dissipated. He switched on the engine and put the car in gear. "By that time I'll be dead."

"I KNEW ALL ALONG you could take care of this," Eliott Gregory expounded to Sam, smoking his cigar, ignoring that the smoke was drifting toward Caryn's face. The man's narrow-eyed glance took in her set features. "While you may be a good magazine editor, Caryn, I don't think you could have handled the heavy stuff all on your own. You still have a lot of growing up to do. Maybe this taught you a lesson, though. From now on be careful what you print."

"With Jenkins it wouldn't have mattered." Sam stepped in. "If it hadn't been Caryn's article it would have been something else. He had to blame his misfortune on someone, and she was the easiest target. Luckily his hired thug was willing to talk, once he realized his boss wasn't about to stand behind him."

"Still, it was Caryn's article that started the whole mess," the older man pointed out.

Caryn looked down at the veal, with a cream sauce she had scraped off. Exotic French cooking had never been her favorite, but when the big boss came to town and insisted on taking her and Sam out to dinner, they had no choice but to go along.

"You know, Sam, I could use you in the main office," Mr. Gregory told him. "Just name your price and I'll move you out right away. This office seems to be in order and you can choose who can take over for you. This would mean a nice promotion."

Caryn's head snapped up at the announcement. Sam looked at her with the barest of smiles on his lips before turning to his boss.

"No thanks. If it's all right with you I'd rather stay here."

The older man looked from one to the other and grunted. "Well, maybe you can teach her some sense."

Caryn put down her fork. "Mr. Gregory, you have spoken over my head all evening as if I'm some kind of dimwit who can't string two words together," she said in a deceptively mild voice, although her eyes fired off deadly sparks. "If you think I'm so unsuitable for the job why did you give it to me? I've heard you say many times the only way you know if someone can handle the challenge is to throw it at them. Fine. Mine has been thrown at me with a vengeance lately. My offices were practically trashed, I have a ruined dress and shoes and I almost lost an eye. Isn't that enough for you? I certainly know it's more than enough for me."

He stared at her for a long time before he burst into laughter. "So the kid has claws after all. The way you've been so quiet I figured you only had dirt for brains, except when it came to that magazine. Who knows, you might make it after all." He applied himself to his meal, leaving the other two people at the table stunned.

"HOW MUCH ALKA SELTZER can I take at once?" Sam groaned when they entered Caryn's town house later. "I feel as if there's a twenty-ton weight inside my stomach."

"It was probably the mousse," she replied, switching on the hall light.

"I thought the French had finally done away with all those heavy sauces." He followed her up the stairs and headed for the bathroom. A moment later he came out with a glass of fizzing liquid and drank it quickly.

"Some restaurants still believe it's the only way to cook." Caryn took off her copper silk dress and folded it neatly before placing it on a chair as a reminder it needed to be dry-cleaned.

Sam walked over and placed his hands on her shoulders. "I'm proud of you." He kissed her bare shoulder and began trailing his lips down her arm.

She smiled. "Because I told Mr. Gregory off?"

"Because you stood up for yourself. Telling him off was merely the icing on the cake. I have a hunch the man's bark is worse than his bite, but I wouldn't care to push the issue."

Caryn turned around and circled his neck with her arms. "After I stood still for the scolding you gave me I had to get a little of my own courage back any way I could." She almost purred under his feather-light caresses.

"If that thug had harmed you, not even the police could have held me back from killing him." Sam's lips found her pulse and traced the blue vein before moving on to each finger.

Wanting him badly, Caryn gripped his hair and pulled his head up. "Now that I've tasted power," she murmured, moving her pelvis against his and noting his instant arousal, "I want it all."

Sam reached down and picked her up in his arms. He walked over to the bed and dragged the quilted comforter from it before lowering Caryn. He shed his clothes in record time and followed her down.

"I always did like these things," he commented, tracing the lace edging of her mocha silk teddy. One by one, the tiny buttons in front were released and the edges spread apart. He lowered his head and fastened his lips onto one of her burgeoning nipples.

Caryn breathed sharply through her nose as the sensations threatened to overtake her. Wanting to share these feelings with Sam, she reached out and touched him with hands of love. It wasn't long before touches weren't enough. Sam cursed the teddy when he discovered it couldn't be removed as swiftly as he liked. Their eyes locked on one another as they began the slow sensual movements that sent them to heaven each time, even though every time they made love they were certain there was something new and exciting about it.

When Sam rolled onto his side, he brought Caryn with him.

"Marry me."

Chapter Seventeen

It was the awareness of being alone in bed that woke Sam up. He blinked his eyes, waiting while they adjusted to the darkness. He noticed the downstairs light was on again and ordinarily would have rolled over and gone back to sleep, but this time he wasn't going to ignore it. Not after the words they'd exchanged a few hours earlier.

"Don't ask me to marry you," Caryn had said in a low heated voice.

"Oh, I'm sorry if I offended you. I just haven't ever asked anyone to marry me before," he said with blatant sarcasm. "I guess I should work on my delivery."

"You don't understand."

"Then enlighten me." All traces of their lovemaking was gone from his face and body language. "Tell me what can be so upsetting that you freeze up when I propose to you?"

Her gaze slid away. "I don't want to discuss it."

"You don't want to discuss it. Fine, just run away like you always do." Sam turned away, so he didn't see her flinch at his words. "You sure have a funny way of showing you love me."

She sat up, clutching the sheets to her bare breasts. "What are you talking about?"

His face was again settled in grim lines. "Easy. We've already decided we love each other, we get along pretty well, so the next logical step is marriage."

"Not for me!" she shouted. "It wouldn't work."

"How do you know it wouldn't?" he yelled back. "Have you had that many previous marriages that you consider yourself an expert?"

"Because!"

"Because what?"

But Caryn refused to say anything further. When Sam finally settled under the covers she showed surprise as if she had expected him to get up and leave. He was glad he could throw her off balance, even if it was only because of something that minor.

When Sam awoke the heated words rang in his ears. As he lay under the warm covers something teased his nostrils. The smell of chocolate. Not stopping to think, he pushed the covers back and quietly hunted for a pair of sweatpants he kept in one of Caryn's dresser drawers.

He pulled them on and crept down the stairs, making sure to keep out of sight of the kitchen doorway. He stopped short at the picture before him.

Caryn dressed in a warm robe, sat at the table, which was loaded down with a carton of ice cream, a box of cookies, a bowl of peanut brittle and a microwave pan of brownies in front of her. She ate from each bowl as if there were no tomorrow.

Sam felt a tearing in his gut as he realized exactly what he was seeing. He walked silently down the short hall leading to the garage and, once inside, found the freezer door unlocked. He opened it, looked at the contents and wasted no time reentering the house. He headed for the kitchen where he discovered Caryn walking toward the downstairs bathroom.

"Can't sleep?"

Caryn looked up, her eyes wide with shock. "I, ah, wanted a drink of water. Why don't you go upstairs and I'll be right up."

"There's water upstairs." He took a step to the side, effectively blocking her way. "In fact I feel a bit thirsty, too. Why don't we get it from the kitchen." He took her arm and began leading her back the way she had come.

"No! I can bring some up to you." She felt frightened, hanging back from him.

"Nonsense," Sam said firmly. "There's no reason to do that." He stopped in the doorway, looking at the littered table. "Funny, I never thought you went in for junk food all that much." His eyes speared her motionless.

She shivered under his relentless gaze. "Every woman gets sweet cravings," she muttered, vainly trying to pull away from his viselike grip.

By now his patience was gone. "Stop it, Caryn. I've figured everything out."

"Figured what out?" she bluffed.

He spun her around and grabbed her shoulders. "I saw the freezer. I saw you in there a moment ago eating like a starving woman. Don't try to act as if I don't know what I'm talking about." The anger rose in him. "Why? You, of all people, should know better. Is this the kind of image you want to give your readers?" he demanded. "Are you trying to kill yourself? That's what happens to a lot of people. In fact, how far are you into this?"

Something else occurred to him. He released her and started toward the downstairs bathroom.

"No!" Caryn screamed, trying to stop him, but he brushed her off.

A search of the bathroom cabinet netted the prescription bottles and over-the-counter drugs.

"What are you trying to do to yourself?" he demanded, holding up the bottles and reading the labels before snapping them open and dropping the contents in the commode, flushing them away.

"Stop that!" Caryn reached out, but Sam easily evaded her. "You have no right to do that."

"I have every right. I'm not about to stand by and watch you kill yourself."

"You have no idea what you're talking about," she said haughtily, crossing her arms in front of her, but her entire body trembled and her eyes refused to meet his.

"Don't I?" Sam felt sick inside but he forced the anger in his soul to keep the sickness at bay. "Perhaps you would like me to spell it out for you. You're bulimic, Caryn. I believe it's called an eating disorder. You stress yourself out, so you binge on food just as you were doing a few minutes ago, and I'd say you were on your way in here to purge yourself."

Caryn's eyes glittered with fiery lights, but she still couldn't look at him. "You're crazy."

"Am I?" He walked out of the bathroom, afraid of touching her again. He spun on his heel and looked at her with mixed emotions. "Why?" he wondered out loud. "You exercise more than enough, you watch just about every bite you eat, at least in public. So why do you go through all this? Are you that afraid of gaining one ounce? Why are you trying to kill yourself?"

"Stop it! Just stop it!" Caryn clapped her hands over her ears. Tears spilled down her cheeks.

But he wasn't about to let up. He gathered her into his arms and rubbed her back in slow long strokes. "Caryn, I love you. Tell me what to do to help you," he murmured in her ear, her pain echoed in his voice.

By now she was sobbing. She flung her arms around his neck and rested her cheek against his chest.

"Caryn, honey, please don't. You'll make yourself sick," Sam pleaded. When her tears refused to cease he picked her up and carried her upstairs. He placed her on the bed and went into the bathroom, coming back with a damp cloth, wiping away her tears.

"You don't understand," she cried, curling up in a fetal position. "You eat all you want and don't gain an ounce while I have to count every mouthful. The doctor told my dad it was just baby fat and it would soon go away, but he didn't believe him so he told me to lose it or else." She opened her eyes, silently pleading with him to understand. "Don't you see? I had no choice."

Sam cursed under his breath, feeling his rage now directed elsewhere. He sat down by her side, gently rubbing her back. "There're other ways, Caryn. You know that."

"Why can't you just let it rest? Now do you see why I won't marry you? In fact, you're probably relieved I turned you down," she said bitterly. "You'll just walk away now that you know. Just the way my fiancé did."

"You honestly think I'm going to walk out on you because of this?" He was incredulous. "Damn you, look at me!"

Her hair whipped around her shoulders. "Yes," she hissed. "So just leave me alone. I already know how vile I am."

Sam was quickly discovering there was more than one man to be angry with. He leaned back, disbelief etched on his features as it all sunk in.

"So that's why the guy broke your engagement," he mused. "He found out and left you. Obviously it wasn't pretty."

"He walked away just as I know you will. So just go." Caryn twisted away.

"Is that what you want me to do? Leave you?" Sam asked quietly.

Her reply was muffled by the pillow she hid her face in, but he recognized the nod of her head.

"You want me to get up, get dressed and walk away so you can say all men are alike? That they only give you love when you're perfect and take it away when you make a mistake? Sorry, but you lose this time." He pulled her upright. "Because you're stuck with me."

Sam shook his head with frustration.

"You're serious," Caryn breathed, finally realizing there wasn't any disgust written on his face, only love.

"Like it or not, we're in this together," he informed her. "But there's something you have to do for me. I want you to call Dr. Milford first thing in the morning."

She lifted her head. "You're asking the impossible."

"Am I? Caryn, we're getting married. We're buying a house with the picket fence and maybe a dog and station wagon, although I don't intend to give up my Mustang and I wouldn't expect you to give up your Porsche—only drive slower. You're not going to be doing this alone," he vowed. "All I want you to do is talk to the man. Will you do that for me?"

She kept shaking her head. "You don't understand. It's young girls who have this problem."

"Not according to the good doctor," he reminded her. "He said career women do, too. I'm not crazy enough to think you'll do it for me. You have to do it for yourself."

She stroked his beard-rough cheek. "I do love you," she whispered. "I was just so afraid you'd hate me for—"

"Suffering from bulimia," he finished for her. "No, but I hate what it will do to you. You're a very strong woman and I'll be with you every step of the way, if you'll let me."

Caryn pressed her fingers against her lips. "You would actually do that?"

He groaned. "You are the most stubborn woman I have ever met. How many times have I said I loved you? Yes, I'll do anything to keep you with me for the next fifty years. Please do something before you land in the hospital from complications. They say love is a pretty powerful medicine. Let's test out the theory."

Caryn chewed on her lower lip. "If we're going to get married, could we set the date for a few months off?" she said hesitantly. "I want to give you an out."

"If it will make you feel better we'll do that only if I can give up my place and move in here," he suggested. "Think of the rent I'm wasting by keeping a place I'm never in."

"The others—Tami, especially—will hate me." She felt helpless, with all the barriers falling down around her.

"They adore you and they'll understand," Sam assured her. "I'm sorry, baby, but you've just run out of excuses. I mean it. I won't pressure you into something you're not ready for."

Caryn sat up straighter. "For the longest time I've feared that you'd find out and turn away from me. Every time I thought I was losing control I could handle it this way. They say it isn't easy."

"What *is* easy?" He smiled, all this love for her shining in his eyes.

She looked uncertain. "And all I have to do is call Dr. Milford in the morning?"

"Yes."

Caryn thought for a moment, then slowly nodded.

Sam took her in his arms. He knew that was the first step, and he was willing to help her all he could.

"Sam?" She said his name in a small voice.

"Mmm?"

"Will you do something for me?"

"Anything," he vowed.

"Stop smoking. They say that can kill, too."

He released her and got out of bed. After rummaging through his pockets he withdrew a pack. Opening the window he tossed it outside.

"We'll help each other," he told her, holding out his hand.

Caryn slid off the bed and walked over to him, wrapping her fingers around his hand. "Yes, we will."

CHRISTMAS IS FOR KIDS

AMERICAN ROMANCE PHOTO CONTEST

At Harlequin American Romance® we believe Christmas is for kids—a special time, a magical time. And we've put together a unique project to celebrate the American Child. Our annual holiday romances will feature children—just like yours—who have their Christmas wishes come true.

A reddish, golden-haired boy. Or a curious, ponytailed girl with glasses. A kid sister. A dark, shy, small boy. A mischievous, freckle-nosed lad. A girl with ash blond braided hair. Or a bright-eyed little girl always head of the class.

Send us a color photo of your child, along with a paragraph describing his or her excitement and anticipation of Christmas morning. If your entry wins, your child will appear on one of the covers of our December 1989 CHRISTMAS IS FOR KIDS special series. Read the Official Rules carefully before you enter.

PROOF OF PURCHASE

AMERICAN ROMANCE

OFFICIAL RULES

1. Eligibility: Male and female children ages 4 through 12 who are residents of the U.S.A., or Canada, except children of employees of Harlequin Enterprises Ltd., its affiliates, retailers, distributors, agencies, professional photographers and Smiley Promotion, Inc.

2. How to enter: Mail a color slide or photo, not larger than 8½ × 11″, taken no longer than six months ago along with proof of purchase from facing page to:

> American Romance Photo Contest
> Harlequin Books
> 300 East 42nd Street
> 6th Floor
> New York, NY
> 10017.

Professional photographs are not eligible. Only one entry per child allowed. All photos remain the sole property of Harlequin Enterprises Ltd. and will not be returned. A paragraph of not more than 50 words must accompany the photo expressing your child's joy and anticipation of Christmas morning. All entries must be received by March 31, 1989.

3. Judging: Photos will be judged equally on the child's expression, pose, neatness and photo clarity. The written paragraph will be judged on sincerity and relationship to the subject. Judging will be completed within 45 days of contest closing date and winners will be notified in writing and must return an Affidavit of Eligibility and Release within 21 days or an alternate winner will be selected.

4. Prizes: Nine Prizes will be awarded, with each winner's likeness appearing on a cover of our December 1989 CHRISTMAS IS FOR KIDS special series. Winners will also receive an artists signed print of the cover. There is no cash substitution for prizes. Harlequin Enterprises Ltd. reserves the right to use the winner's name and likeness for promotional purposes without any compensation. Any Canadian resident winner or their parent or guardian must correctly answer an arithmetical skill-testing question within a specified time.

5. When submitting an entry, entrants must agree to these rules and the decisions of the judges, under the supervision of Smiley Promotion, Inc., an independent judging organization whose decisions are final. Sponsor reserves the right to substitute prizes of like substance. Contest is subject to all federal, provincial, state and local laws. Void where prohibited, restricted or taxed. For a winner's list, send a stamped self-addressed envelope to American Romance Photo Contest Winners, P.O. Box 554, Bowling Green Station, New York, N.Y. 10274 for receipt by March 31, 1989.

Photo-2

You'll flip . . . your pages won't!
Read paperbacks *hands-free* with

Book Mate • I

The perfect "mate" for all your romance paperbacks

Traveling • Vacationing • At Work • In Bed • Studying • Cooking • Eating

Perfect size for all standard paperbacks, this wonderful invention makes reading a pure pleasure! Ingenious design holds paperback books OPEN and FLAT so even wind can't ruffle pages — leaves your hands free to do other things. Reinforced, wipe-clean vinyl-covered holder flexes to let you turn pages without undoing the strap . . . supports paperbacks so well, they have the strength of hardcovers!

Pages turn WITHOUT opening the strap.

SEE-THROUGH STRAP

Reinforced back stays flat.

Built in bookmark.

BOOK MARK

BACK COVER HOLDING STRIP

10˝ x 7¼˝, opened.
Snaps closed for easy carrying, too.

Available now. Send your name, address, and zip code, along with a check or money order for just $5.95 + .75¢ for postage & handling (for a total of $6.70) payable to Reader Service to:

Reader Service
Bookmate Offer
901 Fuhrmann Blvd.
P.O. Box 1396
Buffalo, N.Y. 14269-1396

Offer not available in Canada
*New York and Iowa residents add appropriate sales tax.

BM-G